A HAPPY PLACE

Shani Smith

*This book is dedicated to all those who pursue
their goals in the face of adversity.*

CONTENTS

CHAPTER 1

Saturday morning

Kema is awakened by a thunderous sound. She leaps out of her bed. *Where is Victor?* The sound couldn't be from a storm because the sun is gleaming through her window. Kema hears a clanging sound. Is it coming from the kitchen? She opens a drawer in her nightstand and pulls out a stun gun. As she walks down the hall, the smell of bacon and freshly brewed coffee fills up her nostrils. Kema breathes a sigh of relief and lowers her stun gun as she enters the kitchen and sees Victor. He is rapidly mixing something in a bowl. Her granite countertop and tile floor have batter and bacon grease splattered over them. Though Kema shakes her head she isn't annoyed. If anyone else was in her kitchen making a mess and not cleaning up immediately, it would bother her.

Victor sees Kema as he turns from the counter and walks toward the refrigerator.

"Hey baby, I hope you're hungry. I'm making breakfast."

"Victor, you were about to get acquainted with my stun gun from all the noise you were making. But, that's so sweet of you. What's on the menu?"

Victor laughs and says, "I'm sorry that I frightened you. "Bacon, scrambled eggs, pancakes, coffee for me and mint tea for you."

"I ran out of mint tea ..."

"I know, I checked before I started cooking and went to the store."

Kema walks over to Victor and says, "You're spoiling me

1

and I love it! Don't change up on me." Victor gently reaches for her hand, pulls her close to him as he wraps his arms around her body and says, "I enjoy seeing you happy, and I won't change."

Victor bends his head down and meets Kema's awaiting lips. She suddenly loses her appetite for food as they kiss.

Kema thinks, *I can't give in again. He'll think I'm insatiable. Push away from him and enjoy breakfast.*

As if Victor heard her thoughts, he slowly removes the arm that is wrapped around Kema's waist, takes her hand and guides her to the kitchen table. He pulls out the chair for her to be seated.

"How many pancakes would you like?"

"Three, please."

"How many scrambled eggs?"

"Two"

After making the pancakes and scrambled eggs, Victor removes the bacon that he placed in the oven to warm. He prepares Kema's plate first and sets it on the table. Then, he hands her a cup of mint tea. He makes his plate and joins Kema.

Victor is about to start eating breakfast, but Kema reaches for his hand and says, "Let us pray. Dear Lord, thank you for the food we are about to receive and bless the hands that have prepared this meal. Forgive us our transgressions as we are not perfect and you know our hearts. In Jesus name we pray, amen."

Kema tastes the eggs first then the bacon and pancakes and thinks, *this man can really cook!*

"Victor, who taught you how to cook like this?"

"My grandfather. He always made breakfast for all the grandkids whenever we would stay at my grandparents' house. I was always the first of the grandkids to wake up and I would go into to the kitchen to watch him cook. He told me one day, '*Boy, instead of standing in the corner watching me do all the work come over here and let me show you how to crack an egg.*'"

Kema chuckled and said, "It sounds like your grandfather didn't play around when it came to cooking."

"You're right. After I learned how to scramble eggs, he let

me fry the bacon and make pancakes for the family."

"I can't wait to find out what else you can cook."

"Now, Kema, don't get too excited. I only learned to cook breakfast. For lunch and dinner, I only heat and serve the food."

Kema and Victor laugh and Kema says, "Okay. Mr. Heat and Serve, how are your kitchen cleaning skills?"

Victor pauses before he replies, "Well, I don't enjoy cleaning the kitchen as much as I enjoy cooking breakfast."

Kema looks back at the countertop and the floor with batter splatter and replies, "I see. I'll give you the benefit of the doubt and clean the kitchen since you prepared such a delicious breakfast."

"I cook breakfast and you clean; we make a mighty good team."

*

Ever since Victor asked Kema out on a dinner date, they have spent every moment of their free time together. During dinner, Kema was all business when she asked Victor to help with Sweet Daddy's Fashions Fashion and Talent Show. She suggested that he ask his law firm, Douglas, Jones and Burr (DJB), to be one of the event sponsors. Kema handed him a one-page document, which highlighted the benefits of sponsorship.

Victor scanned the document and read, "Increase brand visibility, cultivate a positive reputation, interact with prospects...You have done your homework about the benefits. I will present this document tomorrow to one of the partners."

Kema laughed and replied, "Thank you! I'm glad that I understood the assignment."

Victor narrowed his sultry eyes at Kema, extended his hand across the table towards Kema and said, "Now that we have got the business out of the way, tell me why a man has not made you, his woman."

This question took Kema off guard. She didn't know whether to be flattered or annoyed by his inquiry. With a coy smile, Kema slapped his hand away and replied, "Let's get an understanding. I don't need a man to select me to feel like I'm worthy."

Victor leaned back in his chair and said, "Forgive me. That was an idiotic comment. I meant to say that you are beautiful and I'm happy that you are on a date with me and not another man."

"This comment may have guaranteed you another date," Kema replied and they both laughed raucously. As promised, Victor presented the one-page document to DJB, and the firm was interested in learning more about the event. Kema gave a fifteen-minute presentation to DJB, and afterwards the firm decided to sponsor the entire event. Kema was elated that she did not have to obtain additional sponsorship.

With only two weeks to prepare for the event, Victor worked with Kema four hours every day after work and ten hours on the weekend. Kema was amazed at how well she and Victor worked together. Victor volunteered to be the Master of Ceremonies for the event. Kema thought that he would be great in this role because of his welcoming and engaging personality.

The day before the event, Victor secured city permits to hold the event on Benjamin Daniels Way, the block recently named in honor of Kema's father. Food trucks selling Italian beef sandwiches, pizza, tacos, fried chicken and cupcakes lined the block. The aromas coming from the food trucks caused people to form long lines outside of each truck before and during the event. Sweet Daddy's Fashions provided the wardrobe for the contestants, which they modeled before showcasing their talent. Victor captivated the audience with crowd participation chants and by providing a personalized introduction for all ten acts. The winner of the event was selected based on the intensity of the crowds' cheers. Denise Lewis, who sang at Kema's father's funeral, was the crowd favorite and won the competition by singing Whitney Houston's song, *I Have Nothing*.

The event united the community and brought publicity to Sweet Daddy's Fashions and DJB. After the event, Darron, Sweet Daddy's Fashions Assistant Manager, told Kema that

Sweet Daddy's Fashion's Instagram was filled with messages from people inquiring about when the next event would be held. Kema thought that this would be a one-time event. However, she knew that she could not have her small team be responsible for planning the event the following year. She needed to hire an event planner.

Victor recommended Monique Ewing whom his professional network used for their monthly networking events. Kema and Darron met with Monique and were impressed that she could provide a VIP reception for the contestants and fans along with planning, logistics and social media marketing for the event. Kema needed time to go over the proposal provided by Monique. Once she agreed to a contract with Monique, Kema called Victor.

"Hey Victor! Guess what? I've signed Monique as the event planner!"

"I told you she is great."

"Yes! How am I ever going to thank you for all of your help?

Victor takes a moment to reply, then says seductively: "I'm sure we can think of something..."

CHAPTER 2

Monday morning

Time spent with Victor over the weekend reduced Kema's anxiety about her Monday morning meeting with Mr. Reynolds and the other managing directors. She reminisces about their weekend during her drive to work as she sings along to Jill Scott's *The Way*.

Kema catches herself and thinks, *girl, focus. This is Monday morning and you have to get back to the real world.*

The song is interrupted when she receives an incoming call alert from the dashboard of her car. It's her mother, Janice.

"Good morning, Mama"

"Is this my long-lost daughter? I haven't heard from you all weekend. I was calling to see if you were alright?"

"I'm fine, just driving to the office."

"What did you do all weekend?"

"I ran a couple of errands and relaxed."

"You relaxed so much that you couldn't spend Sunday with me? Sunday was Women's Appreciation Day at the church and Sister Lillian asked me when you were coming to church again. You know people start to talk when they don't see you for a while. She asked me if you had a man …"

"Mama, I'm sorry to cut you off. I'm driving into the parking garage at work and I want to say goodbye to you before the call drops. I'll call you when I get home this evening."

"Okay, baby. Have a good day."

Kema guiltily ends the call two blocks away from the parking garage.

Kema says a quick prayer of repentance.

Lord, forgive me for lying to Mama. You know I didn't want to hurt her feelings and tell her I didn't care about what Sister Lillian had to say about my life. You know I'm trying to focus for work. The story about Sister Lillian will have to wait. Help me to choose the right words to say so I will not lie to Mama to spare her feelings. Amen.

*

When Kema arrives at work, she goes immediately to the conference room for the 9:00 a.m. meeting. She arrives at the meeting fifteen minutes early to get a good seat at the conference table. However, there are six managing directors already seated. Wendy Sullivan, managing director of technology, motions to Kema to sit in the chair beside her. Kema smiles and sits down.

"Good morning, Kema. How was your weekend?"

"Great! How was yours?"

"It was fantastic! My husband, kids and I traveled to Iowa to visit his parents. Saturday, we took the kids to the Linwood Cemetery for the Haunted History Walk. On Sunday morning, I bought the cutest needlepoint kits at an Arts and Crafts Festival. Do you want to see what I made with one of the kits?"

Wendy doesn't give Kema time to answer as she digs deep into her Coach bag and pulls out what looks like a blue fabric ornament in the shape of a car.

"That's amazing Wendy! You did this after you came home from Iowa?"

"No, actually I worked on it while my husband was driving us back to Illinois. Finished up after putting the kids to bed. Needlepoint is such a relaxing hobby. It brings me to my happy place. You should try it."

"I don't know if I have the patience or time for a hobby now. Most of my time is spent learning my new position."

Wendy nods sympathetically before saying: "Don't worry, I felt the same pressure two years ago when I started. It gets easier. Trust me. You'll need a hobby or some kind of escape from the job stress."

Kema smiles guardedly then turns toward the conference door when she hears Trevor Reynolds, the CEO of Resilient Financial, entering.

"Good morning, everyone. I hope you are well rested from the weekend. We all have plenty of work to do so I'll keep the meeting brief. The primary mission of our mergers and acquisitions department is to provide our services to emerging sectors in the economy. As you'll recall, Farzeen Patel was supposed to head up our new Fast Fashions sector team but what you don't know yet, is that she's just resigned!"

The people around the table are murmuring softly.

"Yes, you guessed it. This is one vacancy that can't wait to be filled, and you have all demonstrated flexibility and ingenuity in your work. But Ms. Kema Daniels stands out for the integral part she played in Flemings International Foods's successful acquisition of Unbelievable Foods. That's why I'm pleased to announce her as the new managing director of the fast fashions sector team."

The conference room is filled with thunderous applause. Kema is stunned and her surroundings suddenly feel surreal. She has only been working in her new role as managing director of food and agriculture for a month. Now she will have to learn an entirely different sector. Kema thinks, *managing director of the fast fashions sector team? Will this be a conflict of interest with my partial ownership of Sweet Daddy's Fashions? Maybe not, because the store sells urban apparel and not fast fashion. I'll have to consistently check our inventory.*

Once the applause diminishes, Kema says, "Thank you, Mr. Reynolds and fellow managing directors. I look forward to this new challenge and will reach out to you for mentorship."

Wendy gently touches Kema's arm and says, "Let's have lunch soon. I'm sure I can answer some of the questions that you may have."

Kema quickly looks at her schedule on her company phone. "How about 12:30 p.m. today?"

Wendy laughs, "I did say soon but didn't specify how soon ... We can meet from 12:30 to 1:00 today. I have a 1:30 but it doesn't require me to prepare for it. Let's meet at Café Delizioso across the street."

Kema breathes a sigh of relief. "Thank you, Wendy."

*

Kema arrives at Café Delizioso one minute before the agreed meeting time. Wendy is already seated at a table working on her latest needlepoint project.

"Hello, Wendy! Have you been waiting very long? We were supposed to meet at 12:30 p.m., correct?"

"No worries Kema, I was able to arrive fifteen minutes early."

Kema and Wendy order their food at the café counter. Once they are seated, Wendy gives Kema background information on Farzeen's sudden departure from the company after seven years.

"Farzeen worked in acquisitions and mergers of the materials sectors. You know, materials like chemical, mining, oil, and natural gas companies. I was told that Farzeen loved challenges and had expressed interest in becoming the new managing director of acquisitions and mergers of the technology sector; but, the board of directors wanted to pick someone who didn't have any prior experience as a managing director at the company.

"Really, I would have thought the company wanted a manager familiar with the company culture," Kema replies.

"No, they wanted someone who had a background in technology and fortunately I fit the criteria. I was the Chief Information Security Officer of Vivant Cybersecurity, where I had been involved with several mergers and acquisitions. I read an article in a trade association newsletter about Resilient Financial expanding to the technology sector and sent a direct message to Mr. Reynolds on LinkedIn. stating that I was interested in exploring opportunities with Resilient Financial. He replied that he was impressed with my LinkedIn profile and told me to send my resume. After two interviews with the board, I received an offer for the position.

"You have had an interesting journey to obtain this position."

"My first week was rocky. All the managing directors greeted me warmly during my first managing directors except Farzeen. A managing director invited me to lunch after the meeting and told me that Farzeen had been vying for my position. During lunch I was told that Farzeen expressed her dissatisfaction with not being selected and she was offered managing director of the fast fashions sector team. She initially said that she would accept the position; however, a day after accepting, Farzeen submitted her letter of resignation."

Wendy finally pauses her story and says, "Kema, I know that I have told you a lot. You just need to concentrate on acquiring fast fashion clients for the company and start building up your team. Just a heads up, as a test, Mr. Reynolds will suggest the first company for you. Once you acquire that company as a client, it will give you momentum to pursue other clients."

Kema looks at her watch and sees that it is two minutes past one o'clock. "Wendy, I have kept you past our agreed end time. Thank you for speaking with me on such short notice."

"You're welcome Kema; I hope I haven't scared you."

"No, I appreciate your openness," Kema replies.

Kema loses her appetite for the turkey sandwich she ordered. She thinks that this position has entrenched her deeper into office politics than she is comfortable with. Kema also thinks that Wendy is a little too close to Mr. Reynolds and she needs to monitor what she discloses to her.

As Kema and Wendy walk back to the office building, Wendy jumps from one subject to the next.

"My daughter was just accepted to the Midwest Institute for Accelerated Education. I'm so proud of her. My son couldn't get in that school. He spends most of time playing The Legend of Zelda. He picked up the video game playing habit from his father.

You know, I met his father playing video games. Like father like son, I guess..."

Kema is getting a headache from Wendy's excessive prattling. She can't wait to get back to her office for some peace and quiet. Kema musters the strength to say, "Congratulations to your daughter. Sorry Wendy, I must walk a little faster to get back to the building to use the restroom. I guess the water I drank earlier wants to be released."

"I understand. We will talk again soon."

Kema begins walking briskly toward the building; immediately feeling relief that she escaped the awkward conversation with Wendy.

CHAPTER 3

Instead of calling her mother back like she promised earlier in the day, Kema decides to visit her after work.

Kema thinks, *it's the least I can do since I haven't really seen or talked to her in a week.* Kema gives her a quick call to make sure she's home.

"Hi, Mama. I'm leaving work now and wanted to know if I could stop by. Do you need me to bring you anything before I get there? Are you cooking today?"

"No, I didn't cook since you didn't come over this Sunday. I planned on eating a turkey sandwich and just going to bed."

Kema frowns at the thought of a turkey sandwich because it reminds her of lunch today with Wendy.

"I have a taste for some fried chicken. Do you want anything from Bailey's Chicken Shack?"

Janice chuckles loudly. "What? Ms. Health and Fitness is going to eat fried chicken? Yes, bring me a two-piece chicken dinner with potato wedges and green beans."

"Yes, ma'am. I should be there in forty minutes."

Kema knows she shouldn't be eating fried chicken considering that she overindulged on food this weekend with Victor. *Today I only had mint tea and one miserable bite of the turkey sandwich. I'll get back on track tomorrow,* she tells herself.

Kema picks up the chicken from Bailey's Chicken Shack, which is only two blocks away from Janice's house. Janice must have been hungry because she opens the door without Kema using her keys.

"Ooh-wee that smells good!" Janice announces as she relieves Kema of the bags of food and walks swiftly to the kitchen.

"Mama, you must be hungry."

"I'm hungry for this chicken now. I was going to be satisfied with leftovers until you offered to bring me something to eat."

Janice and Kema eat their meal without much talking until they both reach for their respective glasses of apple juice.

"How was your day?"

Kema is relieved that Janice isn't asking about Victor and answers after taking a gulp of juice. "Eventful. I found out that I'm no longer the managing director of mergers and acquisitions of food and agriculture ..."

"Baby, you got laid off today? No wonder you're craving fried chicken!"

"Mama, calm down. I didn't get laid off. Mr. Reynolds made an announcement to the team that I am now the managing director of mergers and acquisitions of the fast fashions sector."

"Why did they change you to a different team?"

"The woman that was supposed to be the managing director resigned suddenly."

"She must have done something to resign from a good job like that."

"I don't think so. I was told that she was unhappy with the company and decided to resign."

"She must have had plenty of money saved up to walk away. I'm just glad that you didn't get laid off. "

"I'm still shocked by the announcement because now I have to get to know another team and become familiar with a different sector."

Janice pauses to think for a moment. "You mentioned fashion, right? Will you have to give up ownership of Sweet Daddy's Fashions?

"I hope not. I just have to check the brands that we carry to make sure the brand doesn't represent a client or potential client."

Janice shakes her head. "Girl, you are playing with your career. I knew it was a bad idea to take partial ownership of your daddy's business. Don't mess around and get fired."

"I don't think I have anything to worry about. Sweet Daddy's Fashions sells urban clothing from primarily minority brands. The fast fashions sector caters to teenage girls and young adults."

"Okay ... You know more than I do ..."

Kema senses the sarcasm in her mother's tone. She knows that her mother always has her best interests in mind but she can be very opinionated. Kema hears her phone ringing in her purse and looks to see who's calling her.

It's Victor.

She pulls out her phone to text him a quick message. Janice sees that Kema's facial expression has softened.

"Who's calling you? Is it Sharon? Tell her that I said hello."

"No, it is Victor."

"Estate Lawyer Victor? Victor who helped you with the fashion and talent show? The event is over ... What does he want?"

Kema tries hard not to look annoyed at Janice's barrage of questions.

"He's a nice guy and he's checking on me."

"Oh, so you two are friends now?"

"Yes, I consider him my friend."

"Okay, baby as long as he makes you happy. I'm happy."

"Thank you, Mama." Kema thinks, w*ow, I got off the hook quickly. The fried chicken must have sedated her. I'll have to bring her a meal from Bailey's Chicken Shack more often.*

Kema doesn't want to make it too obvious that she was anxious to leave to talk to Victor, so she watches an episode of *Real Housewives of Potomac* with Janice before leaving.

Once she gets in her car to leave, she sees that Victor has responded to her text.

I've been thinking about you all day. Looking forward to talking with you before you sleep tonight.

Kema smiles and quickly dances in the driver's seat before she locks the car doors and drives home.

*

After a quick shower, she returns Victor's call. The phone goes to voicemail but he calls her back five minutes later.

"Hello, Kema. I was in the shower when you called."

Kema laughs. "I won't hold that against you this time."

"You're a little feisty tonight. I like that."

"You bring out my feistiness …"

"Do I need to come over to see what else I can bring out?"

Kema pauses and thinks, *this is what I get for being a tease. This man really is trying to come over. I need to get a good night's sleep to keep my mind focused for tomorrow morning.*

"I wish. But I've had an eventful day and I need to prepare for what I have to face tomorrow."

Kema tells Victor about her new role at work.

"That's great, Kema, you'll get to learn a new sector."

Victor then tells her that she needs to reconsider her partial ownership of Sweet Daddy's Fashions. He advises her to speak with the ethics department at Resilient Financial to ensure that her ownership doesn't pose an issue. Kema isn't surprised at his response, considering he is a lawyer. She appreciates his perspective and tells him that she will be careful.

After the call ends, Kema's mind is flooded with various thoughts. Both Janice and Victor suggest that she turn away from Sweet Daddy's Fashions. However, an entrepreneurial spirit has been ignited within her. She enjoys the stability of a job, but listening to Wendy's story about Farzeen, she recognizes that stability comes with compromises to personal ambition. Kema thinks Farzeen is brave for recognizing her self-worth and having the courage to leave the company. Kema wonders if she will be courageous enough to leave Resilient Financial if she feels her talents are no longer valued. Will she succumb to the pressure from family and society to stay in a career for stability and social status?

CHAPTER 4

When Kema arrives at work the next day and checks her email, she notices that Mr. Reynolds's administrative assistant has placed a fifteen-minute meeting on her calendar to discuss the next steps in her transition to her new role. Kema is relieved that the meeting will take place in the morning –the earlier the meeting, the quicker she can continue with her day. Kema is surprised to see Lauren McCullough, Wendy and Mr. Reynolds in the conference room when she gets there. Lauren McCullough assumed Kema's former role as director of acquisitions and mergers after she successfully led the final meeting with Flemings International Foods when Kema was at the hospital with her father.

Wendy greets Kema with enthusiasm.

Mr. Reynolds starts speaking the moment she sits down. "Kema, Wendy contacted me yesterday and told me she would be happy to be your mentor. Therefore, I invited her to join us this morning. Lauren is here because she will serve as acting managing director of acquisitions and mergers in food and agriculture."

Kema tries hard to hide her bewilderment at this announcement as she replies. "Thank you, Wendy for volunteering to be my mentor, and thank you Lauren for stepping in for me as I assume a new role."

Wendy and Lauren smile as if they have each received a humanitarian award.

Mr. Reynolds continues. "Kema, we are proud of your accomplishments and believe you will continue to thrive in this new role. Stellar Apparel is interested in expanding by buying smaller fashion brands and fashion boutiques. Your first assignment will involve traveling to New York City next week to meet the CEO of Stellar Apparel to acquire this company as a client. You'll deliver a thirty-minute presentation and answer any questions posed by the attendees. You must invite the CEO and the board members to a dinner meeting to address any other concerns they may have. Make initial contact with the CEO by calling the CEO's personal assistant to introduce yourself. Once you've set a meeting date, your assigned virtual assistant will provide logistical support for this business trip."

"Kema, I'm here to answer any questions you may have while you prepare for this trip. Once you've finished your presentation, I can review it and provide feedback," Wendy says.

"Great, I really appreciate your support."

Mr. Reynolds says, "Kema, I almost forgot to mention this. Since you will be assuming a new role that currently doesn't have any staff, you will need to vacate your office by close of business this week to allow Lauren to move into it. You'll be allowed to work remotely to prepare for your trip to New York City. Don't worry about meeting with your team to tell them of your change in duties. Lauren has graciously volunteered to do that for you this morning."

Kema thinks she is being ambushed. *What's happening here? How can Lauren rapidly obtain a leadership position that took me years to acquire? And how can I focus on preparing for a major meeting* and *clean out my office?*

Kema decides not to question Mr. Reynolds and says, "Thank you, Mr. Reynolds."

She shakes hands with him, Wendy and Lauren before leaving the conference room.

The outcome of the meeting is not what Kema envisioned. She thought she would have a one-on-one meeting with Mr. Reynolds during which he would outline her responsibilities and inspire her to go above and beyond the call of duty. The meeting left her feeling overwhelmed and confused. *Are Lauren and Wendy conspiring against her?* She returns to her office with a pounding headache. Kema usually drinks chamomile tea when she has a headache; however, the tension she is feeling now requires something stronger. She reaches into her desk drawer and pulls out a bottle of ibuprofen. Kema takes two tablets with a cup of water and massages her temples. She closes her eyes and lays her head down on her desk for fifteen minutes then contacts Greg Norman, the office manager, to see if he can acquire five boxes for her to pack up her belongings.

Kema is a minimalist and always keeps her office neat. While Kema was growing up, Janice and Granny Pauline insisted that she kept her surroundings clean and organized. She would be a multi-millionaire right now if she received a dollar each time, she heard Granny Pauline recite the hackneyed expression "Cleanliness is next to Godliness" and Janice say "Clutter is nothing more than postponed decisions." Their nagging about cleaning and organizing irritated her back then; however, now she is grateful for it. Greg appears at her office five minutes later with the boxes.

"Ms. Daniels, I have your boxes. Are you being evicted? You just got here …"

Greg's attempt at humor irks Kema's fragile nerves; however, she won't let him know that his comment bothers her and she sarcastically replies, "Yes, I'm being evicted because I didn't pay my rent."

Greg laughs heartily, showing his toothy smile. "Don't worry Ms. Daniels. You are a resourceful lady and I'm sure you'll land on your feet. Let me know if you need anything else."

Greg's response causes Kema to smile to herself and think, *yes, I am resourceful. With the help of God, I can get through this.*

Kema packs up the belongings in her office in less than an hour and it takes her two trips to load her car. Fortunately, she didn't see any of her staff while moving her belongings. Kema figures that they are in a meeting with Lauren. She receives peculiar stares from the security guards in the building, but they don't ask her any questions.

When Kema arrives home, she only brings in the box that contains her laptop. She figures when she takes a break after three hours of working, she can retrieve the remaining ones. Kema contacts Stellar Apparel CEO's administrative assistant and schedules a meeting and follow-up dinner. Kema then contacts her virtual assistant to make travel arrangements. Kema is grateful that her virtual assistant found a flight next Wednesday, which is a day before the scheduled meeting. Kema breathes a sigh of relief. That's done. She stands, stretches, walks past a mirror in her hallway and catches a glimpse of herself and thinks, *oh, my goodness, I need to call Sharon to see if I can get a hair appointment for next Tuesday.*

Kema hasn't seen or spoken to her best friend Sharon since Sweet Daddy's Fashions Fashion and Talent Show. Sharon and her team volunteered their services by doing the contestants' hair and makeup. During the event, Victor kept announcing that the lovely hairstyles worn by the contestants were courtesy of Gracious Cuts Beauty Salon. Ever since the event, all three of her salon locations have clients on their waiting lists. Kema knows that Sharon doesn't do hair often because she has focused her attention on expanding her salons; however, Sharon always makes an exception for Kema.

Kema calls Sharon's cell phone and leaves a message. Later that night, Sharon sends her a text saying that she can do her hair and have the nail technician work on her nails next Tuesday at 4:00 p.m. After reading the text, Kema feels relieved, turns off her cell phone and falls fast asleep.

CHAPTER 5

The next few days go by in a blur. Kema spends all day Wednesday and Thursday working on the Stellar Apparel presentation. She promised Wendy that she would email a draft of the presentation by Friday morning for her to review before their 2:00 p.m. meeting. Not wanting any surprises before practicing the presentation with Wendy, Kema sends an email to Wendy asking if she is the only person who will be attending. Wendy confirms that she will be the only meeting participant.

Kema arrives at the conference room ten minutes before the meeting and connects her laptop to the projector. Wendy arrives promptly but doesn't look enthused about being there. Kema shrugs it off. *Maybe Wendy is having a bad day?*

"Good afternoon, Wendy. How are you?"

"Hi Kema, unfortunately I'm not feeling very well this afternoon, and I'll be leaving work soon after I listen to your presentation."

"I'm sorry about that. I don't want to keep you longer than necessary. I will begin now."

Kema gives her presentation and Wendy suggests that she shorten the introduction and ensure that her presentation focuses more on how Resilient Financial can simplify the acquisition and merger process for Stellar Apparel. Wendy also tells her that she needs to perform more research on the company so she can tailor her answers to their questions to specifically address their concerns.

What is Wendy talking about? I researched the company and thoroughly performed a market analysis of Stellar Apparel as shown by the graphs in the presentation.

But Kema doesn't refute Wendy's comments. Instead, she thanks Wendy for her time and tells her that she hopes that she feels better soon.

As soon as Kema leaves the conference room, she sees Marsha, her former executive assistant, and Lauren walking in the hallway. Both ladies exchange uncomfortable glances with Kema before Kema speaks to them.

"Hello ladies, how are you?"

Marsha replies first. "Hi Kema, I'm fine … It's good to see you."

Lauren replies. "Hello, Kema. I'm doing well. I've been so busy that I didn't tell you that my team says that you'll be missed."

Kema finds it peculiar that Lauren would use the phrase "my team". From the meeting earlier this week, Mr. Reynolds stated that her role was *acting* managing director. Kema conjures up her best smile and replies, "No worries. I've been working on a presentation this week and would have likely missed your call or email."

"Oh, that's correct. You have a presentation in New York next week. Best of luck!"

Kema ends end this uncomfortable conversation by replying: "Thank you, it was good seeing you both. Have a great weekend."

Kema takes the elevator down to the parking garage. As she walks to her car, she suddenly feels as if she's an outsider at her own company. Kema knew that she would be challenged by taking this new role, but she didn't imagine she'd be ousted from her office. Kema gets in her car, fastens her seatbelt, and tightly grips both hands on the steering wheel. Kema says to herself, *you have a presentation to give and you don't have time to feel sorry for yourself. Focus!*

Once Kema arrives home, she calls Darron and asks him to email her an updated brand inventory list every Friday for Sweet Daddy's Fashions. Darron does this and Kema quickly scans it. She's relieved that Stellar Apparel isn't there. She works a few hours on the presentation and looks at her cell phone that has been placed on "Do Not Disturb" mode. Kema has a missed call and voicemail from Victor. She listens to the voicemail message.

Hey Ms. Daniels! I'm calling to see if you wanted to join me and my colleagues at the Art Institute of Chicago tonight at 7 p.m. for a members-only grand opening of the Augusta Savage exhibition. I know how you feel about last-minute invitations, but I thought I would take a chance. Let me know. Talk to you later.

Kema thinks, *I love that Victor is so considerate of me. If I didn't have this presentation to work on, I would go to the grand opening.* Kema returns his call.

"Hello, Kema. How are you? Can you join me tonight?

"Hi Victor, I'm doing fine. Unfortunately, I'm going to have to take a raincheck. I have a major presentation to revise and practice this weekend. The company is sending me to New York to meet a potential client next Thursday. I'm feeling a bit overwhelmed."

"I'm sorry that you can't join me, but I understand. We all planned to go out to dinner after the opening. Have you had anything to eat? I can pick up something for you."

"No, I haven't. Enjoy yourself. I wouldn't have you come all the way over here to bring me food."

"Don't worry about it. I know you're busy tonight and need a good meal. Just keep your phone close to you."

"Okay ..."

Within fifteen minutes she receives a text message from a food-delivery company stating that a driver is on the way with an order from the new restaurant Authentic Food Company. She casually mentioned to Victor that she wanted to try this restaurant based on the good reviews. Kema laughs out loud and says to herself, "This man is really trying to win my heart!"

Victor has chosen well. The delivery is a grain bowl containing quinoa, salmon, kale, black lentils, dill and is drizzled with a mint yogurt sauce. She washes her hands, grabs a spoon and taste the dish. The salmon is cooked to perfection and the flavor of the bowl is phenomenal. Before she consumes the entire meal, she takes a picture of the bowl. Kema sends Victor a "thank you" text with the picture attached, and under the picture she places a smiling emoji with the tongue sticking out to symbolize that the meal is delicious.

Victor responds fifteen minutes after Kema sent the text. *You're welcome. I wish I could be there with you.*

Kema sees his text, smiles and continues eating. Each forkful of food seems to be better than previous one.

*

Kema works on the presentation all day Saturday and decides she needs to take a break from it on Sunday. She calls Janice on Saturday night and tells her that she will arrive at her home at 10:30 a.m. on Sunday to take her to church. Kema can hear the delight in Janice's voice when she says, "I'm so happy you're going with me this Sunday. If you'd called me earlier today, I would have made a trip to the store to buy food for our Sunday dinner ..."

"I didn't want you to go through any trouble since I can't stay with you all day. But, I want to spend some time with you and hear a message on Sunday to help sustain me through the upcoming week."

"Reverend Wilson is supposed to preach on Sunday. His sermons are always good."

"I hope he has a special message for me. I'll see you tomorrow."

On Sunday morning, Kema's alarm goes off at 7:30 a.m. She showers, makes a cup of mint tea, and dresses. Chicago's weather in October is perfect for layering and Kema puts on a black turtleneck dress, a burgundy leather jacket, and a pair of black knee-high leather boots. This combination perfectly complements her five-foot-eight frame.

Kema picks up Janice and they arrive at the church ten minutes before the service begins. They sit on the fifth pew in the middle aisle of the church in front of Sister Lillian. Sister Lillian has been a member of Greater Love Baptist Church for over forty years and lets the congregation know this during the testimonial portion of the service when she stands and gives a testimony about God's goodness. She is a fiery, petite seventy-five-year-old with a milk-chocolate complexion. Her salt and pepper colored hair is pressed and curled to frame her round face. Sister Lillian reaches over the pew and places her left hand on Janice's shoulder and her right hand on Kema's shoulder. Kema and Janice look back at Sister Lillian and greet her in unison: "Good morning, Sister Lillian. How are you this morning?".

"Good morning, Janice. I'm doing good now that I'm in the house of the Lord. I see you have your daughter with you. Nice to have you with us, young lady. We missed you last Sunday for Women's Appreciation Day. We could have really used your voice in the Women's Choir last Sunday."

Kema gives Sister Lillian a puzzled look and replies, "Thank you for considering me, but I don't sing."

"That's okay, dear. We would have found a place for you to help out. You could have served as an usher or helped cook and serve breakfast after our 8:00 a.m. service."

"Thank you, Sister Lillian. I'll keep that in mind for next year."

Kema is relieved the conversation ends once the choir starts singing *Power Belongs to God* and the church is filled with praise and worship. Pastor Wilson delivers a sermon entitled "Confidence in Jesus Christ" and references the Bible verse, Philippians 4:13, which states: *I can do all things through Christ who strengthens me.* Reverend Wilson also tells the congregation that they can overcome their obstacles by meditating and confessing Romans 8:37 that says: *Nay, in all these things we are more than conquerors through him that loved us.*

Kema feels as if Reverend Wilson tailored the sermon specifically for her and is overwhelmed with tears of joy. She opens her purse and pulls out a tissue to dab her eyes. Janice notices and places her arm around Kema to comfort her. Reverend Wilson ends the sermon and asks those who want special prayer for any situation to come to the front of the church. Kema leaves her seat and walks to the front along with other members from the congregation to receive prayer. Once she returns to her seat after Reverend Wilson's prayer, she feels as if the burden of uncertainty about her new role at Resilient Financial has been removed.

Kema takes Janice back to her home after church then returns to her condo to finish her presentation. She's done just in time to watch one of her favorite reality shows. Kema only watches the first thirty minutes of the show before falling asleep on the sofa. She's awakened by the loud insurance commercial with the pig leaning its head out of the window screaming "wee". *Time for bed*. She feels fortunate that her bedtime routine doesn't involve deciding what suit to wear to the office the next day.

Maybe working remotely has its benefits.

CHAPTER 6

Kema finishes her workday early on Monday and Tuesday to pack her clothes for the trip to NYC and to free up time for her hair appointment with Sharon. On Tuesday, Kema arrives at the beauty salon and finds that Sharon is waiting for her instead of the other way around.

"Sharon, you beat me to the salon. Is everything okay?

Sharon laughs and replies. "You are a VIP now. I can't keep the managing director waiting. Besides, it's unprofessional to have clients waiting."

"Has my promptness finally rubbed off on you?"

"Yes, best friend, it has. I've always admired that about you."

"Aww. Give me a hug!"

Sharon and Kema embrace and Sharon steps back and says, "I watched as you walked in the door. You seem to have a certain glow. I know this new position isn't giving that to you ..."

"I went to church with Mama on Sunday and Rev. Wilson gave a great sermon on having confidence in God."

Sharon gives Kema an incredulous look before saying, "I know the Lord can give you joy; however, I'm sensing the joy of the Lord sprinkled with some happiness from a man. How is Victor doing?"

Kema can't hide anything from Sharon. She thinks like a detective. Kema smiles and says, "Victor's doing fine. He's been so thoughtful. I told him that I couldn't spend time with him on Friday night because I was working on the presentation. This man surprised me and had food sent to me from the Authentic

Food Company! Can you believe it?"

"Girl, what I can't believe is why you didn't go over to his house that night and surprise him with a 'special delivery'."

Kema laughs loudly and replies, "Sharon, you're so crazy. I don't have time for that. I need to stay focused for this trip."

"I know. You've always been responsible. I just want to know one more thing."

"What's that?"

"Does he have a successful single brother? I'll also take a successful single cousin, uncle, nephew ..."

Kema and Sharon continue catching up as the nail technician gives Kema a manicure. Sharon talks Kema into getting a gel manicure instead of her usual French. Kema chooses a pale pink color that compliments her amber skin tone. She is pleased with her nails and hair and feels confident in her appearance.

*

It's Wednesday morning and Kema is packed and ready for her trip to NYC. She requests a driver on a ride-hailing app to take her to the airport at least two and a half hours before her flight. Kema believes it's better to be at the airport extremely early instead of rushing to the gate to make the flight. Kema uses the extra time at the airport to catch up on her reading and to people watch. Her flight is scheduled to depart at 9:00 a.m. and arrive in NYC at noon. This will give her enough time to get settled in her hotel room and find a nice place to eat for lunch. She plans to eat a light dinner tonight because she doesn't want to sleep on a full stomach before her presentation in the morning.

Kema looks up from her book and checks the clock at the gate. 8:40 a.m. No announcement has been made for passengers to board. Kema thinks that the flight must be delayed for a few minutes and continues reading. She looks up again at the clock: 9:15 a.m. Now she is getting concerned. Kema thinks that if the flight is delayed until the afternoon, she'll still be okay.

At 9:30 she hears the following announcement over the PA.

"Attention passengers. Flight 2589 from Chicago to New York City has been cancelled due to a mechanical malfunction of the plane. The next available flight is Thursday at 10:00 a.m. We apologize for any inconvenience."

This is unbelievable. I won't make it to the 11:00 a.m. meeting on time if I take the flight on Thursday. There has to be another flight today out of Chicago.

Kema calls her virtual assistant.

"I'm sorry Kema. All the flights from Chicago to New York City are overbooked today. There's a technology convention in New York."

"Can I be placed on standby for one of the flights?" Kema asks.

"You can. But you'll need to stay at the airport and there's no guarantee that a seat will become available. Would you like me to reschedule the meeting with Stellar Apparel?"

"No, don't reschedule the meeting. I'll call Mr. Reynolds and explain the situation."

Kema ends the call, takes a deep breath, then calls Mr. Reynolds. Her call goes to voicemail and she has to leave a message.

Three hours have passed and Mr. Reynolds has not returned Kema's call. Kema calls the administrative assistant of the CEO of Stellar Fashions and explains the situation. She then asks if she could give a virtual presentation to the CEO and attendees. The administrative assistant tells her that she'll ask and let her know.

After an hour she calls back and confirms the virtual option. Kema immediately pulls out her laptop and schedules the meeting using Adobe Connect. She calls her virtual assistant to let her know the change in plans and then leaves another voicemail for Mr. Reynolds.

During the ride back home, Kema thinks that at least she doesn't have to worry about adjusting to the one-hour time change or the hotel noises as she sleeps. She was looking forward to the in-person interaction with the Stellar Fashions CEO and the board members. Also, since she wouldn't have to return until Saturday, she'd planned to be a tourist and hop on a double-decker tour bus for a tour of New York City. Kema vows that next summer she will take a weekend to visit. Maybe Victor would go with her? If not Victor, maybe Sharon? Kema stops herself from thinking so far in the future and starts rehearsing the presentation in her head.

Once she arrives home, she checks her work email to see if Mr. Reynolds chose to respond to her by email instead of calling her back. Nothing is there from him, but she does see an email from Wendy.

Kema,

I'm sorry I didn't provide written feedback on your presentation. Let me know how the meeting goes tomorrow.

Wendy

Kema thinks this is just a method for Wendy to monitor her work but call it "mentoring". Kema thought this new role would give her more independence, but it seems like there are people behind the scenes making decisions for her.

Mr. Reynolds calls Kema at around five.

"Ms. Daniels, I received your messages regarding the change in plans for the presentation tomorrow. I have confidence that you will represent our company well during the virtual presentation. Is there anything you need from me?"

"Thank you for returning my calls. I believe I have everything I need for tomorrow's presentation."

"Very good. I look forward to hearing your report on Monday. Have a good evening."

Kema exhales deeply after pressing the "end" button on the cellphone. She is relieved that Mr. Reynolds didn't question her decision. Now that Kema has heard from Mr. Reynolds, she feels that she can enjoy a meal. She read that eating foods rich in omega-3 fatty acids, vitamins, and minerals the night before a presentation is beneficial. Kema prepares salmon, wild rice and spinach. After eating, she practices her presentation for two hours before going to sleep.

*

It is 6:00 a.m. on Thursday and Kema is in the kitchen drinking water before her thirty-minute jog on the treadmill. She always feels more confident and ready to take on challenges after a good session. Afterwards, Kema takes a shower and prepares a cup of tea before logging on to her computer. She checks her work email to see if there is anything she needs to handle immediately. There are no new emails in her inbox and she breathes a sigh of relief. As she leaves her desk to walk to her bedroom closet, her cellphone rings. Kema thinks, *who could be calling me this early?*

It's Darron.

"Hello, Ms. Kema. I called to tell you that we received a shipment of new inventory on Wednesday and I've already updated the inventory spreadsheet. I know you requested that I send the updated spreadsheet on Friday, but I'm not working this Friday. Can I send you the spreadsheet today?"

"Yes please. Thank you for letting me know."

Darron is very efficient. I hope that my tone wasn't too harsh when I answered the phone. Should I check my email and look at the spreadsheet before the presentation? No, I can't have any more distractions. Kema sets a reminder on her phone to check the email on Saturday and says a quick prayer: *Lord, calm my anxious mind.*

CHAPTER 7

Thirty minutes before the presentation, Kema clips a ring light to her laptop and adjusts the lighting. She checks her small condenser microphone to ensure her audio is working properly. Kema runs her hand across the sleeves of her coral blouse as if to smooth away her nervousness. Although she has presented multiple times during her career, she still feels anxious until she begins speaking. Once she starts, it's like a switch turns on and she channels all her nervous energy into the presentation.

Kema logs in to the video conference and turns on her laptop camera. Olivia Crenshaw, a petite thirty-three-year-old fashion designer who is CEO of Stellar Apparel, greets Kema and introduces her to Stellar Apparel's board members. After the introductions, Kema begins. Sure enough, Kema feels at ease while presenting and the thirty minutes goes by quickly. By the stern look on Mrs. Crenshaw's face, Kema cannot determine if she is receptive to working with Resilient Financial. Nevertheless, she eloquently answers Mrs. Crenshaw and the board members' questions.

Mrs. Crenshaw finishes the meeting as she says, "Thank you, Ms. Daniels for your presentation. We will deliberate and you will hear from us by next Wednesday."

Kema turns off her microphone, camera, and exits the video conference. She is relieved that the presentation is done. While the meeting is still fresh, she begins drafting her summary report for the Monday meeting with Mr. Reynolds and the other managing directors. After an hour, she takes a break and sends Wendy an email letting her know that the presentation went well. A few moments later, Kema's work cell phone rings.

Wendy.

"Hi Kema, I hope I didn't catch you in the middle of something. I'm glad the presentation went
well. I heard that Olivia Crenshaw can be really tough. Did she pepper you with questions?"

Kema thinks, *I told her that the presentation went well. What more does she want to know?* She pauses before speaking to ensure her voice does not reflect her aggravation. "I think her questions were reasonable considering that her company will be paying for our services if Stellar Apparel becomes our client."

Wendy replies with disappointment in her voice because Kema did not engage her with further details about the meeting. "Very well, then … Congratulations on completing your first presentation as a managing director. I can't wait to hear your summary on Monday."

"Thanks, Wendy for your support. Have a good day."

"Thanks, Kema, have a great one."

Kema smiles at how she was able to diplomatically handle Wendy's inquiry about the presentation. Kema's excitement has subsided and now she feels hungry. She makes a smoothie with strawberries, banana and almond butter and figures it will sustain her through the end of her workday. Kema works until five in the evening and logs off the computer. Although it's Thursday, it feels like a Friday to her. She wonders what Victor is doing tonight and sends him a text. After ten minutes, Victor calls her.

"Hello Victor."

"Hey, lady. I'm glad that you answered. I hope I'm not disturbing you. I decided to call instead of text so I could hear your sexy voice."

Kema's body starts to heat up and she thinks, *uhh ohh! I have started something now by texting him.* Kema replies, "I love it when you call me. What are you doing tonight?"

"I have to meet with clients tonight. Are you available tomorrow?"

Kema jokingly replies, "I'll have to check my schedule and get back to you."

Victor chuckles, "Okay, have your people call my people as soon as they know."

"You know what just happened? My assistant must have been eavesdropping on our conversation because she just whispered to me that I am available at 7:00 p.m. on Friday."

"My people just told me that 7:00 will work for me as well. I remember you saying that you'd like to learn salsa dancing. There's a beginner's salsa dance class at Caliente Nights Dance Studio at seven on Friday. After the class we can order food and sip on drinks on the G. Barker rooftop."

"Mr. Pennington, it sounds like you have put a lot of thought into this. I look forward to dancing, dinner and drinks with you on Friday."

"I had to step my game up because I'm dating a managing director at Resilient Financial."

"Is that so? I appreciate your attentiveness. I hate to think where you would take me if I wasn't so important," she jokes.

"Nothing much would change except we'd have a Wednesday night date consisting of dinner at Bailey's Chicken Shack and dancing at the Player's Den."

"Why Wednesday night?"

"Wednesday night is Ladies' Night at the Player's Den and ladies get in free."

Kema and Victor laugh heartily.

"That is so wrong. I guess I should ensure I retain my position if I want to experience high quality dates with you," Kema replies.

"Just continue to be the high-quality woman that you are.

Hey, I stepped outside to talk to you and I have to get back inside. I'll text you the address of the dance studio. Talk to you later."

Kema shakes her head and smiles. The last time a guy made her smile like that was during her freshman year at DePaul University. Kema met Chris Thompson in the library while she was studying for her final exams. Kema usually sat at a single desk tucked in the corner of the library; however, on that day all the single desks were filled. Kema was sitting at a long table, which had space enough for three other students and leave a chair open between them. Chris sat down in the seat next to Kema and she looked up at him questioningly.

As if he read her mind, he smiled at her and said, "Oh, were you saving this seat for someone? If so, too bad you're stuck sitting next to me now. My name is Chris. What's yours?"

His absurdness took Kema off guard and she couldn't help but laugh and replied, "I'm Kema. I can move to another table."

Chris rustled through papers in his backpack and replied, "Good luck with that, darling. The library is getting crowded and I doubt that you want to hunt for another seat."

By this time, the three students sitting at the table started giving Kema and Chris dirty looks.

Kema looked up and noticed how full the library was. "You're right, Chris. Could you lower your voice before you get us both kicked out?"

Chris walked Kema back to her dorm room that night and she found out that he was a second-year theatre arts major from St. Louis, Missouri who aspired to act and direct Broadway plays. Kema and Chris became good friends and he would invite her out. Chris was unapologetically boisterous and the life of every party. You would always find him in the middle of the floor hyping up the partygoers and moving his lanky, six-foot-two frame to the beat of almost every song the DJ played. Kema would often join him before any other people would feel comfortable enough to dance.

After Chris graduated from DePaul University, he moved to New York City to pursue his acting career and they lost contact. Kema had hoped that during her business trip that she would see his name on a huge sign on a Broadway theatre or in one of the playbills.

Kema finishes her summary report early Friday afternoon to prepare for her Friday night date with Victor. She wants to look fabulous. Fortunately, her hair is still in good shape and she only needs to add a few curls in the front with a curling iron and touch up her edges with a light gel. Her gel manicure is still intact and she only needs to paint her toenails and do her makeup. Kema decides to wear a black wrap dress accessorized with silver earrings, necklace, bracelet, red clutch purse and black peep-toe heels. A few sprays of Dolce and Gabbana perfume and she is ready to go.

Kema arrives at Caliente Nights Dance Studio ten minutes before the class starts and is greeted by the receptionist who directs her up the stairs and right to enter the dance studio. When she walks through the door, she is surprised to see Victor has already arrived and is chatting with a tall, thin Hispanic woman wearing a red body suit and a black skirt. Victor is looking handsome as usual and is dressed in a white button-down shirt, black slacks and black patent leather dress shoes. They stop their conversation once they hear Kema approach them.

"Hola, you must be Kema. My name is Griselle and I'm your instructor tonight."

"Nice to meet you Griselle."

"Victor requested a private lesson for you tonight. We will start with basic individual salsa footwork before you dance together."

Griselle positions herself in front of Kema and Victor to demonstrate front and back salsa basic and side salsa basic footwork.

There is a large wall mirror in the front of the studio that allows Kema and Victor to observe their movements. Kema and Victor quickly learn the footwork and Griselle teaches them the cumbia basic footwork before teaching them how to incorporate their footwork with a partner.

Kema gently places her hands in Victor's as he leads her through the basic partner footwork.

"Have you taken salsa lessons before?" Kema inquires.

"I have but it has been about two years. I was going to ask you the same question but then I remembered you saying you had never taken lessons."

"We're just talented dancers."

Victor leads Kema into a right turn and then he turns himself.

Kema laughs. "Now, you're just showing off."

Griselle laughs and says, "Once you and Victor have a few more lessons you both could help me teach my beginning salsa classes."

"We just may take you up on your offer," Victor replies.

CHAPTER 8

After the salsa lesson, Kema and Victor have food and drinks at G. Barker. It's an unusually warm October night and they are able to sit outside on the rooftop bar, which is crowded with other patrons also enjoying the good weather. The DJ is spinning an eclectic mix of pop and hip-hop music from the early 2000s. Kema and Victor bob their heads to the music while eating, drinking and watching people dance who seem to be attempting to converse with their friends over the blaring music.

Later, Victor walks Kema to her car and asks if she wants to come over to his place. Although he has come to her home a couple of times during the two months they have dated, Kema has never seen where he lives. She thought that he would eventually extend an invitation to visit his home. Tonight is the night.

He texted her his address and she put it in Google Maps. He lives in the South Shore neighborhood about a twenty-five-minute drive from G. Barker. Kema knows the area well because she took many field trips to the South Shore Cultural Center as a child. During the summers at the center she was allowed to explore dance and visual arts through their youth program. Kema is not surprised that Victor lives in the South Shore. He always wants to stay connected to the plights of African-Americans and he has stated on multiple occasions that living in the community will facilitate this. Kema loves his cultural awareness and imagines that his place will be filled with African-American or African artwork.

Kema secures a parking space behind Victor in front of his three-unit building. Kema and Victor hold hands as they walk together and climb the stairs to his third-floor condo.

"Bienvenida a mi casa, Kema," Victor says.

"Gracias, Victor, I see you know a little Spanish ... A man of many talents."

"Not as talented as the lady standing before me. How do you manage to take my breath away every time I look at you? If I keep looking at you, you'll have me speaking another language."

Kema laughs and replies, "Just make sure you have an interpreter with you if you do."

"I'm being a bad host. Please sit down. Can I get you anything to drink?"

"Some water please."

"I'll be right back."

Kema sits down on his dark brown sofa and sinks into the cushions. Kema thinks, *how old is this couch? I don't want to think about how many people have been on this sofa.* After adjusting her body on the couch, she turns her head to the right and looks up at the picture hanging nearby. It looks like an abstract oil painting of two men in African tribal attire. One man is standing prominently in front of the sand landscape while the other man is standing in the background. Besides this one painting, there is no other artwork on the walls. In the middle of the coffee table, there is a sculpture of a man climbing the stairs and a woman sitting at the top. Kema smiles and thinks the sculpture is symbolic of Victor's approach to dating: he puts in every effort to obtain favor from a woman.

"One glass of water for the lady," Victor announces as he hands Kema the glass and sits next to her.

"Thank you, you are such a good host."

"Anything for you..."

Kema and Victor's conversation flows effortlessly from one topic to another. Victor tells her about how he became interested in becoming an estate lawyer. Victor was seventeen when his grandfather, Papa Joe, died without a will. Over the years of working in the meat-packing plant in Chicago, Papa Joe saved enough money to purchase land in Mississippi that his family used to work as sharecroppers. Victor said Papa Joe kept telling the family that they would inherit the land in Mississippi should anything happen to him. Unfortunately, Papa Joe succumbed to prostate cancer and the family had to battle probate. During the probate proceedings, three children came forward from Papa Joe's previous marriage to a woman in Mississippi. Victor's grandmother knew that Papa Joe was married before but he'd never mentioned that he had children. This revelation caused much hurt and confusion in the family and Victor decided that he wanted a career that would help families avoid this. He read about the best majors for students interested in going to law school. Victor majored in economics at the University of Illinois in Chicago and earned a law degree at Loyola University School of Law.

"Now I understand your passion for your profession," Kema says.

"Law school wasn't easy. I didn't want to be loaded with debt once I finished my degree so I worked as a law clerk for Schuman & Lancaster. After I graduated, I thought they would hire me. But they decided to hire Jacob Schuman, the great-grandson son of the founding partner, Nicholas Schuman. After about a week moping around my mother's house, I applied to DJB and have become indispensable."

Victor shifts his back to the arm rest of the couch and embraces Kema.

Kema laughs. "You really think you are indispensable?"

"I've been there since I was twenty-four and now I'm

thirty-eight. I've mentored new attorneys, brought new business and facilitated community involvement. Next year, I plan to apply for partner."

"I see. I'll need to make plans for a celebratory party."

"Yes, start preparing now." Victor takes his right hand and touches Kema's chin as he moves his head to kiss her. Kema doesn't resist and they kiss and caress each other. Feeling things were going to the next level, Kema slowly moves her body away from him.

"Where's your bathroom?"

"Second room on the right."

Kema finds the bathroom and turns on the light and notices the pedestal sink has soap stains but no soap. The toilet lid is covering the toilet and she is afraid of what she will see once she lifts the lid. She holds her breath and counts to five before she lifts it. The toilet bowl has a black film and she is unsure if it is mold or an accumulation of hard water. Not wanting to sit down, Kema hovers over it to urinate quickly.

Kema thinks about digging in her purse to find hand sanitizer but decides to open the shower curtain to see if at least Victor has some bodywash she can use to wash her hands. She pulls back the shower curtain and reaches for a sliver of green soap in the shower caddy. Kema looks down at the faucet and notices a pair of black lacy panties hanging from it. Kema gasps and it must have been loud enough for Victor to hear.

"Hey, Kema are you alright?"

"I'm fine. I hit my elbow on the doorknob."

Kema takes the sliver of soap and washes her hands and dries them on a towel that is hanging on a wall hook. She exits the bathroom and takes a deep breath in the hall. *Why is a pair of panties hanging in his bathroom? Obviously, he's dating someone else and didn't bother checking and cleaning the bathroom. Pull yourself together. Look like everything is fine.*

Kema walks back into the living room and Victor is still seated on the couch, smiling with his shirt off and his thighs involuntarily moving back and forth in anticipation of Kema sitting between them. Any other time seeing him with his shirt off would have enticed Kema. Kema musters a polite smile and says, "I'm going to head out. Thanks for inviting me to stop by."

Victor gives her an incredulous look before replying, "Do you really need to leave? I thought we were enjoying our evening. Let me take a look at your elbow. Maybe I can kiss it and make it feel better."

"I need to get a good night's rest because I have plenty of errands to run early Saturday morning."

"Okay … next time we need to spend the weekend together. Spending only a few hours with you is just not enough. I'll put my shirt and shoes on."

Victor walks Kema to her car. When he moves his face close to hers for a good night kiss, Kema quickly turns her head and the kiss lands on her cheek.

"Kema, what's going on? Your mood changed when you went to the bathroom."

Kema looks at him with her head tilted and says, "You didn't have soap on your sink so I looked in the shower to find some soap and saw a pair of women's underwear."

Victor lowers his head, curses under his breath, and looks up at her and says, "Come back upstairs with me and I can explain everything."

CHAPTER 9

"I don't know if I want to hear this explanation tonight. It appears you are seeing someone else as well."

"I'm not seeing anyone. Please come back up and let me explain."

Kema reluctantly walks back upstairs with him. When she enters his condo, she stands close to the door with her arms folded and says, "Victor, this is looking like you want to date several women at one time and I'm not into sharing my man. I'm looking for an exclusive committed relationship."

"I want what you want. Listen, someone came back from my past and needed a place to stay. I didn't check the bathroom … I'm so sorry."

"It seems that you have a lot of unresolved relationship issues. Contact me once you get it together."

"Kema!"

Kema sprints out of his condo, bounds down the stairs to her car and speeds off. She bites her bottom lip to prevent the tears from falling and obstructing her vision. Kema was blinded by his charm and ignored the warnings her mother gave her when she first met him. This incident with Victor is a wake-up call. Kema thinks, *I shouldn't have let him get so close to me. Time to redirect my energy.*

Once Kema arrives home, she feels the urge to call someone to decompress but reconsiders when she notices that it is past midnight. She goes to the kitchen and makes a cup of chamomile tea. She takes the tea to her bedroom, lights a lavender and mint-scented candle, and turns on the tub faucet.

The sound of the water splashing in the tub soothes her nerves. Kema sips her tea in the tub and feels so relaxed that she almost forgets where she is. She finishes her bath, dries off, and falls fast asleep as soon as she says the Serenity Prayer.

God grant me the serenity to accept the things I cannot change, the courage to change the things I can, and the wisdom to know the difference.

*

Kema wakes up early Saturday morning thinking about Victor and decides that working up a sweat will take her mind off him. Instead of running on the treadmill, she works out to a kickboxing routine streamed through her television. With each front and side kick, Kema feels aggression and anxiety leaving her body. After her workout, she sends Sharon a text to see if she has time to meet for dinner later tonight to catch up. Kema knows that Sharon is very busy now that she owns the three beauty salons but she is hopeful that she can spend a couple of hours with her. Sharon returns Kema's text and suggests that they meet at seven at the Maiden on the Boat restaurant. Kema accepts Sharon's restaurant choice and Sharon texts her with the reservation confirmation. Feeling satisfied that her evening has been planned, Kema showers and dresses to run some errands.

Kema returns home at around four, which gives her enough time to get ready to meet Sharon. She feels "casual chic" will be the theme of the night and puts on a silver long-sleeve cold shoulder mock neck sweater, skinny jeans and black leather knee high boots. As she is walking out the door, her cellphone begins to ring. *Sharon calling to say she's running late?* She looks at the phone and sees it's Victor calling her. Kema sighs and lets his call go to voicemail. Once she gets in the car, she receives an alert that he left a voicemail. Not wanting to be distracted by it, Kema searches her music app for a song and decides to listen to *Nice for What* by Drake, starts her car, and drives to the restaurant.

Kema enters Maiden on the Boat before seven and it is crowded, which is typical for a Saturday night. The restaurant is a fantastic prelude for a night on the town because of its upbeat music, creative cocktails and appetizers. Kema looks around the restaurant and mostly sees ladies dressed in bodycon dresses and a few gentlemen dressed in button-down shirts and slacks, who appear to be in their twenties. They're laughing loudly at the bar in anticipation of the night's adventures.

Kema thinks, *oh to be in my twenties again. How would my life be if I hadn't spent most of my twenties studying and working to-*wards *the next promotion?*

Before Kema has a chance to ponder this question, Sharon saunters into the restaurant.

"Hey Kema! Look at you girl ... I'm loving your outfit. I feel underdressed. Do you have a date after our dinner?"

"Not at all... I felt like I needed to step it up to keep up with you. You know you always leave the house as if you are on a fashion-model runway."

Sharon looks around the restaurant and also notices that the bar area in the restaurant is filled with young men and women. "Well, I know one thing is for certain, as good as we look, we can give these little girls a run for their money."

The hostess leads Kema and Sharon to their table. They quickly scan through the menu and order their food and drinks when their waiter arrives at the table. Sharon looks across at Kema with a smile and says, "The last time I talked to you, you were getting ready for the big presentation in New York City. How did it go?"

"Well. I had to give a virtual presentation because my flight was cancelled and I couldn't get another flight to New York City that would get me there on time."

"Too bad you missed the Big Apple. So ... you haven't mentioned Victor. How's he doing? I hope he's working on hooking me up with one of his good-looking colleagues, brothers, or cousins."

Kema didn't think Sharon would mention Victor so soon. She thought that she would have had at least had one cocktail before discussing him. Her face must have shown her distress.

"Oh no. Don't tell me he's messing up already. What did he

do?"

"We went out last night and had a great time until I went to use his bathroom and saw panties hanging from the bathtub faucet."

"Panties? He didn't bother to check his bathroom before inviting you to his place? That is trifling."

"He claimed that 'someone from his past' needed a place to stay."

"Oh, so his place is a bed and breakfast? I hope you don't believe his story."

"I told him that he needs to address his unresolved relationship issues and to contact me once he has."

"Whoa ... You left the door open for him to contact you again? This situation would be a dealbreaker for me and I'd have blocked his number."

Kema looks skeptically at Sharon and thinks, *listen to her go. This is the same woman who gave her ex-boyfriend, Tony, so many chances before finally breaking up with him.*

"Technically, we didn't say we were exclusive. I take part of the blame for assuming we were exclusive, based on the consistent attention he has given me. I figured with his work schedule he didn't have time to date anyone else."

"Girl, you've been out of the dating game too long. Men always find time for what they want. It sounds like what he wants is to see other women. Has he tried to contact you?"

"He called right before I left my place, but I didn't answer."

"Good. He needs to know that if he has options, you have other options too!"

Their food and drinks arrive and the conversation ceases as they share small plates appetizers of buffalo shrimp, mini crab cakes and margherita flatbread. Each time they go out they make a pact to drink two cocktails: one they are familiar with followed by an unfamiliar one. Kema and Sharon both like vodka cocktails and the first one they drink is called "Bossy". The second cocktail they try has a gin base and is called "The Exhibitionist". It's much stronger than "Bossy".

"Whew. Maybe we should have reversed the order that we consumed these drinks," Kema says before reaching for a glass of water.

"Don't tell me you're already tipsy. Three drinks used to be our limit. But I can't lie, this last drink has me seeing stars. Bottoms up!" Sharon replies and then also drinks a glass of water.

Kema and Sharon finish their appetizers and decide to take a short stroll along the bustling Chicago Riverwalk. Couples are walking hand in hand as if they have been in love for an eternity. It reminds Kema that she has yet to find that type of romantic love. Maybe taking a walk on the Chicago Riverwalk on a Saturday night was a bad idea. A gust of wind hits both Kema and Sharon in the face and reminds them that it is still an October night in Chicago and they decide to call it. Luckily, they are parked in the same parking garage and are able to walk together.

"Thanks for hanging out with me tonight, Sharon."

"You know I have to make time for my bestie. Promise me that you won't let that Victor get the best of you."

"I promise. Text me when you get home."

As soon as Kema gets in the car, she gets an alert on her phone. Kema thinks, *please let it not be Victor*. She looks at her phone and notices that the alert is the reminder that she set to check the email that Darron sent with the inventory spreadsheet attachment. Kema breathes a sigh of relief as she puts the phone back in her purse and drives out of the parking garage.

When Kema arrives home, she immediately opens her laptop to check the email. She opens the spreadsheet and observes that the clothing brand names are not in alphabetical order. Kema selects the column containing the clothing brand names and sorts the column in descending order. The twenty-fourth clothing company listed on the spreadsheet is Stellar Apparel.

Kema's stomach drops as if she is descending on a rollercoaster.

How am I going to explain this to Mr. Reynolds?

CHAPTER 10

It is Monday morning and Kema arrives at the office one hour before her ten o'clock meeting with Mr. Reynolds and the managing directors. She is exhausted from ruminating all Saturday and Sunday night about telling Mr. Reynolds about the conflict of interest that she will have if Stellar Apparel decides to become a client. Kema chooses not to disclose it. She's relying on the expression her mother and Granny Pauline used to use when they didn't want to worry about a future outcome: "I'll cross that bridge when I get to it." Now that she no longer has office space, Kema goes to the café in the building lobby until it is time for her meeting in the conference room.

At twenty to ten, Kema gathers her belongings and takes the elevator to the sixth floor. Kema opens the conference room door and sees that no one has arrived yet. She removes her laptop from her bag and connects it to the projector. Kema logs into her laptop and uploads her presentation. As soon as the title slide appears on the screen, several managing directors including Wendy Sullivan enter the conference room. Kema exchanges pleasantries with each managing director until Mr. Reynolds enters the room.

"Good morning, everyone. I hope you had an enjoyable weekend. We'll start our meeting with a brief presentation given by Kema Daniels."

Kema gives a ten-minute presentation, which includes information on how Resilient Financial performs due diligence research on the seller's company throughout the merger and acquisition process. Kema describes how Resilient Financial will continuously review Stellar Apparel's enterprise strategy to ensure that it is aligned with its merging and acquisition strategy. In addition, Kema states that she gave an overview of the elements of the integration plan provided to the buyer before each merger and acquisition deal is closed. Kema asks if anyone has any questions and Wendy raises her hand.

"Kema, in your presentation to Stellar Apparel, did you discuss how Resilient Financial will observe the company cultures of the buyer and seller to ensure that the merger will be beneficial to both companies?"

"No, I didn't include it in my presentation and no one from Stellar Apparel raised this question."

"This should have been integrated in your presentation. It could make the difference between obtaining or losing a client."

Kema is momentarily taken aback by Wendy's abrasive tone and the fact that Wendy helped her finalize the presentation without mentioning this issue. She smiles and responds tactfully. "Thank you, Wendy for your feedback. I will implement your suggestion in my next presentation."

There is an uncomfortable silence in the room before Mr. Reynolds stands up and says, "Thank you, Ms. Daniels for your meeting summary. I have an announcement regarding Ms. Daniels to make."

Kema's stomach feels as if it is turning flips and she has the sudden urge to go to the restroom. Kema thinks, *why does Mr. Reynolds always make announcements to the group that affect me?*

Mr. Reynolds continues. "Olivia Crenshaw, the CEO of Stellar Apparel, called me this morning and said that she looks forward to working with us. Stellar Apparel is now our client. Let's congratulate Ms. Daniels on acquiring her first client as a managing director!"

The room erupts in applause and Kema turns to Mr. Reynolds and shakes his hand. As Kema walks to her seat, she notices that Wendy is not clapping but looking at something on her cellphone.

After the applause ends, Mr. Reynolds says: "I have nothing further to discuss ... Have a productive day, everybody."

Mr. Reynolds approaches Kema as she is disconnecting her laptop from the projector. "Ms. Daniels, please schedule a meeting with me this week to discuss your strategy for Stellar Apparel. Now that you have a client, you'll need a team to assist you. Wendy can be a resource on team selection. Once you have a team, we can discuss office space in the building. I look forward to hearing what you have in mind."

"Will do, Mr. Reynolds."

Kema gathers her belongings to return to her home office. She thought that she would have had more time to think about how she would tell Mr. Reynolds about her problem. Now she has to have this conversation immediately.

*

Instead of playing music in her car, Kema rides home to the sounds of traffic. While at a stoplight, she reaches for her cellphone to call Victor to get his advice. However, Kema remembers the promise that she made to Sharon about not contacting him. Kema rationalizes that if she contacts him, she will keep the conversation professional. Who is she fooling? Once she hears his voice, she will want his advice *and* an explanation of the panties hanging from the faucet. Before she presses the "call" button under Victor's name, the stoplight changes to green.

Once Kema arrives home, she logs on to her work computer and checks Mr. Reynolds's schedule. She sees that he is available from 11:00 a.m. until 12:00 p.m. the next day and 9:00 a.m. to 10:00 a.m. on Thursday and selects the first time slot. Kema thinks, *it's better to have this difficult conversation earlier in the week rather than later.* An hour after submitting the meeting request, Kema receives an automated email stating her requested meeting time has been approved. There is no turning back now.

Now that Kema has scheduled the meeting, she shifts her focus on how to tell Mr. Reynolds. Kema knows that her facial expressions show her emotions, so she decides that she needs to practice her conversation with Mr. Reynolds in the bathroom mirror. Each time she practices, she ensures that her shoulders are not raised and her tone of voice exudes confidence. Overall, Kema's interaction with Mr. Reynolds has been positive. She imagines that once she tells him that he will be supportive and reassign her to another managing director position within Resilient Financial. Perhaps she can return to her former team as the managing director Kema thinks, *I will persuade Mr. Reynolds that I will be more effective as managing director of food and agriculture than of fast fashions.*

As Kema pulls back the comforter on her bed and is about to climb in the bed, her cellphone rings. It's Victor. Kema thinks, *he must have felt me thinking about him earlier today.* She lets his call go to voicemail. Kema flops her head on her pillow and stares at the cellphone for about a minute as she decides whether or not to call him back. She can't resist the urge to call him and presses the "call" button.

"Hello?" Victor answers the phone as if he has been gasping for breath.

"Hello, Victor. I saw that you called."

"Kema, how are you? Can we talk about the other night?"

"I'm not ready to talk about that, but I do need your advice on another issue."

"Okay …What's up?"

"Tomorrow morning, I have to tell Mr. Reynolds about my conflict of interest at Sweet Daddy's Fashions."

"Wow … So, you confirmed that you have an issue?"

"Yes, Darron sent me the inventory spreadsheet and a company that is a Resilient Financial client is on the list."

"Well, have you thought about selling your share of the business back to Linda?"

"No, she wouldn't be interested in buying my share because she wants to step away from the business. After I tell Mr. Reynolds, I will persuade him that my skills are best suited as managing director of agriculture and food."

"What will you do if you can't persuade him?"

Kema pauses before she answers. "I … haven't thought about what I would do. I'm confident that he'll see my point of view."

"Okay … I know you are very persuasive, but from my experience, very few CEOs are willing to move their top performers to other roles because they want to continue their side hustles."

"Being part owner of Sweet Daddy's Fashions is not just a side hustle for me Victor. I'm continuing my father's legacy."

"Look, I'm just playing devil's advocate. I know how hard you have worked to obtain a senior-level position at your company. I also know that you are very organized and efficient and can balance a demanding career with managing Sweet Daddy's Fashions. However, I don't want you to be blindsided if Mr. Reynolds doesn't allow you to obtain your former position. You have to start thinking about your next move."

"I see your point of view. I can't say I agree with it, but I acknowledge it."

"Good, now can we talk about the other night? Kema, I'm —"

"I really must get some rest to prepare for my meeting tomorrow. Can I talk to you later?"

"Oh, okay. Let me know the outcome of the meeting."

"Sure, good night."

Kema ends the call, gets out of the bed, and kneels beside it with her hands folded.

Lord, you know the outcome of this situation. Guide the words that will come out of my mouth and take control of my demeanor. Let me exhibit my God-given confidence. In Jesus name I pray, amen.

CHAPTER 11

Kema gets out of the bed the next morning feeling refreshed. Usually, the night before an important meeting, she has a difficult time falling asleep. Last night was an exception because she fell fast asleep after praying. Kema thinks, *I guess that I did what Mama and Granny Pauline always said to do after praying: don't worry*.

After her morning routine of exercising, showering and dressing, she grabs her laptop bag and heads out the door. Instead of listening to a motivational podcast on her way to work, Kema opens her music app on her phone and connects her Bluetooth. The first song that appears is *Jesus Can Work It Out*. Kema smiles and repeatedly listens to the song during her commute to the office.

Kema arrives at Mr. Reynolds's office ten minutes before the meeting and checks in with his administrative assistant, Brian Davis, who offers Kema something to drink. Kema politely declines and removes her heavy black wool jacket and lies it across the chair beside her. She reaches in her purse to get her cellphone to place it on silent. As she does this, she notices that Victor sent her a text message with a four-leaf clover emoji saying "Good luck". Kema feels pleased that Victor didn't seem to have been offended by her abrupt end to their conversation the previous night. His gesture this morning may make her inclined to listen to what he has to say sooner rather than later. Kema's thoughts are interrupted when she hears Brian's nasal voice on the phone.

"Mr. Reynolds, Ms. Daniels has arrived a few minutes

early. Can you meet with her now? No … Well, yes, I offered her something to drink … Alright … I'll tell her." Brian places the call on hold.

"Ms. Daniels, the meeting that Mr. Reynolds is in now will end ten minutes later than he expected. Would you like to continue waiting or reschedule for another day this week?"

"I can wait. Thank you for the update, Brian."

Brian gives her a half-smile and picks up the phone receiver. "Ms. Daniels will wait for your meeting to end."

Kema repositions her body in the chair and is tempted to open her laptop to check her email but she resists. Kema thinks, *I don't need to get distracted by reading emails. By the time I compose my response to one email, Brian will tell me that I can go into Mr. Reynolds office. No need to look like a fool nervously scrambling to gather my belongings.*

In an attempt to refocus, Kema closes her eyes and takes a deep breath as she repeats to herself: *I can do all things through Christ who strengthens me. This is not a problem, but an opportunity to shine.*

Suddenly, Kema feels a tap on her shoulder. "Ms. Daniels, are you okay? Mr. Reynolds is ready to see you."

"Oh … Thank you Brian," Kema replies while scrambling to pick up her belongings, feeling the embarrassment that she was attempting to avoid.

"Good morning, Ms. Daniels. I apologize for the delay. How are you today?" Mr. Reynolds greets her.

"Good morning, Mr. Reynolds. I'm doing well."

"Great to hear. Let's hear your strategy for Stellar Apparel."

"Before we talk about strategy, I must tell you about a conflict of interest I have with Stellar Apparel."

"Why would you have a conflict of interest? Have you been a consultant for Stellar Apparel?"

"No, I haven't been a consultant; however, I am part owner of my father's clothing store. I just discovered that the store now sells clothing from Stellar Apparel."

"I see … Do you plan to relinquish ownership of your father's clothing store?"

"Mr. Reynolds, I would like to be reassigned as the managing director of food and agriculture."

"Ms. Daniels. I don't think that's even a possibility. We are vetting candidates for this position right now."

"I would welcome the opportunity to be considered as a candidate again."

"I'm sorry. We selected you as the managing director of fast fashions. We don't have the time or the resources to have two open managing director positions. I'm sure you understand."

"Yes, but …"

"Ms. Daniels, it seems that you have a decision to make. You can continue with Resilient Financial by divesting your interest in your father's business. You have been an asset to us for many years. We would be happy to have you continue to grow with us, but, returning to your former responsibilities is not an option. Please let me know what you decide by this Friday."

"Mr. Reynolds … I think—"

"If we aren't discussing strategy, our conversation is over until this Friday. Please speak with Brian to schedule our next meeting. Have a good day Ms. Daniels."

Mr. Reynolds turns away from Kema as if he were a parent who had just disowned his child. Kema is in shock and stands still for a few seconds to gather enough composure to leave the office. She exits so quickly that she doesn't notice Brian smirking at her.

She presses the down button for the elevator and once it arrives, Wendy Sullivan exits the elevator.

"Well, hello Kema. What are you doing on the tenth floor?"

"I just had a meeting with Mr. Reynolds."

"By the look on your face, it looks like it didn't go well. You know you can always run ideas or strategies through me. That's what mentors are for …"

"Thank you, Wendy. I really must be going now."

Kema enters the elevator and thinks, *If I run into one more person, I think I'll scream. Please let me be the only passenger.* Fortunately, her wish is granted and she exits the building without running into anyone else. Once she gets into her car, she takes a moment to breathe. It feels as if she's been holding her breath since she left Mr. Reynolds office.

Kema drives home without listening to anything but the traffic sounds. Once she arrives home, she kicks off her shoes by the door and flops onto the sofa. She remains face down for about ten minutes as tears fall down her face. Kema never imagined that Mr. Reynolds would respond to her in such a frigid manner. Victor had been right. Kema had thought she could speak up for herself during the discussion but nothing had gone according to plan.

Kema pulls herself up from the couch and goes to the bathroom. After washing her face, she looks at herself in the mirror and thinks, *I need a few days off from work to decompress …* Kema has plenty of vacation days since she rarely takes time off work. She pulls out her laptop, logs into Resilient Financial personal time-off system, and requests the remainder of today, Wednesday and Thursday. Suddenly, Kema remembers in her haste to leave the office, she forgot to schedule the meeting with Mr. Reynolds. She calls Brian and sets up a 9:00 a.m.

Kema spends the rest of the day binge watching episodes of *Power*, drinking wine and eating chips and salsa. As she sits up from the sofa to pour another glass of wine, her cellphone rings. It's Janice.

"Hi, Mama."

"Hey, baby. Are you alright? I didn't hear from you this weekend. What's going on?"

"I'm fine. Just a lot of things on my mind right now."

"Like what?"

Kema pauses. She doesn't want to tell Janice about the situation at work, but her mother can always tell when she is trying to keep something from her.

"I'm having some issues at work. I have to make a decision about something quickly."

"Can you talk about it or is it top secret?"

"It's confidential."

"Well, have you talked to God about it?"

"I have."

"Well, everything will work out the way it is supposed to."

"Thank you, Mama. How are you doing?"

"I feel fine, but I'm missing my daughter."

"I'll come over tomorrow afternoon."

"You want me to cook something for you?"

"You don't have to go through the trouble."

"The last time you were here we had fast food. I think I can prepare my baby a home-cooked meal."

"Okay, Mama. I will see you at four tomorrow."

"See you then. Good night."

Kema decides not to pour another glass of wine. She folds the half-empty bag of tortilla chips, puts the lid on the salsa, and carries them into the kitchen. On any other weekday evening, she wouldn't indulge in wine and junk food. She's on vacation. Calories won't count until after vacation.

Kema wraps her hair in a scarf, takes a shower, brushes her teeth, and gets ready for bed. Surprisingly, she hasn't thought about her discussion with Mr. Reynolds. Kema is relieved that Victor hasn't tried to contact her to find out what happened. She isn't in the mood to discuss it with him. To prevent interruptions to her sleep, Kema places her phone on "do-not-disturb" mode and falls fast asleep.

The next morning, Kema wakes up with a slight headache and puffy eyes. She is feeling the effects of the wine and tortilla chips. She walks to the kitchen and prepares a cup of warm water and lemon to flush her system and returns to her bedroom to check her cellphone. Victor called last night and sent her a text following up about her meeting. It's around 7:30 and Kema decides to call him because he's usually getting dressed for work at this time.

Kema explains the situation to Victor. He sounds sympathetic.

"In addition," Kema says. "I need to let him know by Friday if I'm prepared to divest my partial ownership of Sweet Daddy's Fashions."

"Ouch. Seems his mind was made up before you even stepped into his office. What are you going to do?"

"One side of me wants to retain the security of Resilient Financial and divest my ownership of Sweet Daddy's Fashion. The other side of me wants to resign from Resilient Financial and use my skills to grow Sweet Daddy's Fashions."

"You know that operating a business full-time is very risky. Becoming a full-time business owner sounds enticing, but you have to be prepared for a lot of personal sacrifices."

"I know, but I feel that I have made personal sacrifices my entire career at Resilient Financial and now the CEO is giving me an ultimatum without listening to my concerns. I no longer feel that I'm in control of my career."

"I hear you, Kema. This is what happens when you work for big corporations. You have to decide what is important to you. I think you do like the prestige of having a title. Your work ethic and dedication to your job are very attractive. You know, we could be a power couple if you stayed with Resilient Financial since I'm working to be a partner at my firm."

"Really, Victor … a power couple? You just made my work situation about you and me. We still haven't resolved our issues."

"Look, I'm just trying to make you think of all the implications of your decision."

"You have made one decision easy for me."

"What's that?

"My decision to continue a relationship with you. Goodbye, Victor."

Kema hangs up the phone and angrily takes a swig from her cup as if she were drinking wine.

CHAPTER 12

Kema spends the rest of the day cleaning her home before going to Janice's for dinner. Cleaning has always been therapeutic for Kema. It gives her peace, happiness and a workout. Kema needs peace before she sees Janice. Inevitably, their conversation will turn towards work and dating and Kema is having problems in both of these areas. Thinking about Janice giving her advice makes her anxious. She is praying now to remain calm.

Kema showers and drives to Janice's home. When Janice opens the door, the smell of salmon croquettes tantalizes Kema's nostrils. Janice hasn't prepared salmon croquettes in a long time.

Kema thinks, *Mama must have really missed me or she's going to ask me to do something. Either way, I'm going to enjoy this meal.*

Janice also prepared creamed corn, mashed potatoes and green beans. The meal is so good that neither Janice nor Kema is interested in a lot of conversation while eating.

"Mama, you really took your time and made this meal delicious."

"Thank you, I know I haven't cooked for you in a while and I had a taste for some seafood. I thought it would be a nice change from chicken."

"Yes, it was. I've I cleaned my plate."

"I see. They must have really worked you so hard at your job that you didn't have time to eat lunch or you have a larger appetite than usual for another reason ... Am I about to be a grandmother?"

"No, Mama," Kema says with a chuckle.

"Okay, so what's going on at work that you didn't have time to eat?"

Kema takes a deep breath before responding to Janice. "I took today and tomorrow off from work to decide if I am going to remain with Resilient Financial."

"Oh Lord, what has happened at that job that makes you want to leave?"

"I have a conflict of interest by being part owner of daddy's store and Mr. Reynolds told me that I need to let him know by this Friday if I will divest my ownership."

"Kema, you should have told him right then and there that you would divest your ownership. Why draw out this decision?" I'm not sure if I want to divest my ownership."

Janice looks at Kema as if she had just at cursed her. "What do you mean that you're not sure? You've worked too long and hard to obtain the promotion that you have. I think that it's noble for you to want to hold on to your Daddy's little store, but you have to remember that your job pays your bills."

"Mama, you don't understand what I'm going through. Right now, I don't feel like I'm valued by the company."

"They still give you your paycheck on time ... right? A good paying job like yours is hard to find. Stay there until you can find another job."

"What if I don't want another job, Mama? I want to do meaningful work and feel that my efforts are impacting many people."

"You can make an impact by volunteering in your free time. The most important thing is to make sure you can take care of yourself by keeping a good paying job. Kema, how can you impact a lot of people when you are struggling to pay your bills?"

"Mama, you served as an usher in the church on the Sundays – you didn't have to work. You affected a lot of people doing that."

"There were very few Sundays that I didn't have to work. You seem to have forgotten that I struggled many hours in that diner to keep a roof over our heads and food on the table. I made sure you had the resources to work hard in school and then get a good paying job so you wouldn't have to struggle.

"Why do you think I'll struggle running Daddy's store full time?"

"Kema, what do you know about running a business?"

"I did earn an MBA and I have been involved in multiple business mergers and acquisitions for fifteen years now at Resilient Financial. With my experience, I'm pretty sure that I can manage Daddy's store. Besides, if I need advice I can talk with Sharon."

"Sharon owns beauty salons, not clothing stores. You need to think carefully about this decision."

"Mama, I will."

Kema gets up from the table and takes their dishes to the sink. In silence, she washes them, puts the leftover food away in storage containers, and places the containers in the refrigerator. Instead of sitting on the sofa with Janice to watch television, Kema tells Janice 'Good night' and heads back home.

*

Once at home, Kema replays their conversation in her head. Kema loves Janice but she's feeling a little resentful. Janice taught Kema to be an independent woman, yet, dependent on a job for her livelihood. Now that Kema is considering making a living independent from a corporation, Janice isn't happy. Kema has spent most of her adult life making sure that she is financially secure and has placed her happiness on hold. Kema thinks, *I'm thirty-five years old, I don't have any kids, and now I don't have a relationship. There is nothing stopping me from running Sweet Daddy's Fashions full time but me. I'll call Linda in the morning to discuss purchasing her portion of the business.*

Kema wakes up around 5:30 Thursday morning. She decides to do a kickboxing workout through her on-demand streaming service. For every jab, punch and kick she executes, she feels lighter. Linda is an early riser, however, Kema doesn't want to call her too early in the morning. After she showers, she makes a cup of tea and starts a list of pros and cons for leaving Resilient Financial. Kema reviews the list and discovers that she has one more pro than con listed. Kema smiles and thinks, *I can show this list to Mama to demonstrate that I have "thought carefully" about my decision. If I don't have confidence in myself, no one will.* Feeling empowered, Kema calls Linda.

"Hello?"

"Hi, Linda. How are you this morning? Is this a good time to talk?"

"Good morning, Kema. Sure. What's on your mind?"

"Are you still interested in selling your portion of the business?"

"Yes, do you know someone who is interested in purchasing it?"

"I am."

Linda doesn't respond immediately but when she does respond she gasps and says, "Ay bendito!" which means "Oh my God!"

"Linda?"

"Yes, I'm here. Did I hear you correctly?"

"Yes."

"Kema, what made you change your mind?"

"To make a long story short, I'm not feeling fulfilled or appreciated in my career. I realize it no longer serves me and I need to try something different."

"I understand. Have you told your mother about your plans?"

"I discussed this possibility with her last night. She wasn't pleased."

"Kema, although you didn't get to spend much time with your father, he and you are very similar. He wrestled with leaving his full-time job to become a business owner. It wasn't easy for him, but he enjoyed working hard for something that he owned. You have an advantage over him because you have studied business and worked for a corporation. Also, since you have been heavily influenced by your mother, I know you have likely saved up money for emergencies. You are intelligent and observant and I know that you can do anything that you set out to do."

"Thank you, Linda," Kema says choking back tears.

"I'm only telling you the truth. You'll be fine. I will contact Victor Pennington to prepare the paperwork for the purchase agreement."

Kema's heart sinks. How did she forget that Victor could be involved in this deal? Maybe he will recommend another lawyer in his firm to oversee the proceedings. She meekly replies, "Okay, sounds good."

"I look forward to talking with you soon. Have a great day!"

Instead of feeling relieved that she has made a decision, Kema feels uneasy. What was merely thought and speculation a few hours ago is in the process of becoming reality: Kema Daniels, business owner. Now, she has to draft a letter of resignation and present it to Mr. Reynolds tomorrow. Kema searches online for a template resignation letter and after about an hour-long search, she finds one that she modifies to fit her situation.

Kema reads the letter at least ten times before she prints it and places it in a manilla folder inside her laptop bag. Although it is only early in the afternoon, Kema feels her energy is depleted. She walks to the glass sliding door that leads to her balcony. It's a cloudy day, which usually prompts Kema to stay in the house. However, today she feels her energy will be renewed by venturing outside. Besides, it is her last day off from work and she needs to do something relaxing. Kema decides a walk around Montrose Beach and parks close to the dog beach areas.

As she passes by, she observes owners walking their dogs on leashes. As some dogs pass each other, they either bark territorially or sniff each other. Kema smiles to herself and thinks that maybe she should become a dog owner, but then remembers the responsibility and expense and quickly decides against it. She walks for about thirty minutes and finds herself in the

Montrose Bird Sanctuary where she spots a host of sparrows. They are congregated together as if they are planning their activities for the winter. Looking at the birds united together as if they were committed to a mission allows Kema to imagine how she will lead her small team at Sweet Daddy's Fashions. They also remind her of the lyrics to *His Eye is on the Sparrow,* which shows that God sees and protects even the smallest living creatures. This thought gives her reassurance that God knows what she is going through and will provide for her.

Kema works up an appetite while walking and decides to treat herself to a take-out cheeseburger and fries. When she arrives home, she devours her meal and washes it down with a glass of wine. Kema watches television afterwards for an hour before showering and getting ready for bed. After only three hours of sleeping, Kema is awakened by a rumbling in her stomach. *Oh no, maybe I shouldn't have eaten such a heavy meal with wine*, Kema thinks as she leaps out of the bed and dashes to the bathroom. She is shackled to the toilet for over thirty minutes before she is able to wash her hands and leave the bathroom. She goes to her kitchen cabinet where she keeps her over-the-counter medications and finds a bottle of Pepto-Bismol. The expiration date was eight months ago. Kema remembers reading on a Quora forum page that taking expired over-the-counter medication isn't unsafe, but it's just not as potent. Kema thinks to herself, *bottoms up* and holds her nose as she takes two tablespoons of the medicine.

The expired Pepto-Bismol is effective enough to prevent Kema from taking another trip to the toilet. Unfortunately, she isn't able to easily return to sleep because she begins thinking about what her life will be like not working at Resilient Financial. She'll have more responsibilities that may involve restless nights of developing marketing strategy and ensuring she has enough money to pay for inventory and the income for her small team of employees. Kema then remembers the encouragement the Linda provided during their brief discussion and she starts picturing herself succeeding as the CEO of Sweet Daddy's Fashions.

*

Friday morning has arrived and Kema feels a renewed strength. Although she felt distress during the night, it has not placed her on the sidelines. She showers, dresses for work, drinks peppermint tea and leaves her home with her head held high. The traffic on the way to the office is unusually light as if many people have taken the day off. When she arrives at the office building, she doesn't feel anxious about running into colleagues or feel self-conscious about them judging her. She walks past Marsha, her former executive assistant, in the lobby and warmly greets her before getting on the elevator. Inside, Kema opens her laptop bag and removes the manilla folder containing her letter of resignation. Kema arrives five minutes before the meeting. Brian lets Mr. Reynolds know that Kema has arrived and she is allowed to enter his office.

"Good morning, Kema. How are you today? Is that a copy of your strategy for Stellar Apparel in your hand?"

"Good morning, Mr. Reynolds. I'm doing well. No, it is not a copy of the Stellar Apparel strategy. It is my letter of resignation."

Mr. Reynolds face suddenly turns the color of a stop sign and he clears his throat. "Okay. You've decided to keep the share of your father's business."

Kema hands the manilla folder to Mr. Reynolds and replies, "Yes, I have. I would like to thank you for giving me the opportunity to work here for the last fifteen years and investing in me."

"You've served the company well and you'll be missed. Brian will give you a copy of the resignation procedures, which provide instructions on returning your office equipment."

"Thank you, Mr. Reynolds. I hope you have a good weekend."

"Best of luck to you Ms. Daniels."

Kema smiles at Mr. Reynolds and pivots on the balls of her feet out of his office. She stops by Brian's desk and he goes over the resignation procedures with her. After returning the office equipment to the IT staff in the basement of the building, Kema presses the up button on the elevator to access the lobby. As the elevator doors slowly open, she sees Wendy and Lauren inside the elevator and overhears some of their conversation.

"Now that Kema has resigned, you are a shoo-in for managing director of the fast fashions sector team. Mr. Reynolds could make you managing director of food and agriculture *and* fast fashions. The sky is the limit for you, Lauren."

"Do you really think so, Wendy? I ... Oh, hello Kema, how are you doing?"

"I'm doing well Lauren. Thank you for asking. Hello, Wendy."

"Hi Kema, we were just talking about—"

"I hope you ladies enjoy your day," Kema says as she confidently steps into the elevator as Wendy and Lauren awkwardly exit it.

CHAPTER 13

During Kema's drive back home, instead of feeling resentful after overhearing Wendy and Lauren's conversation, she is feeling motivated to make Sweet Daddy's Fashions the best retail clothing store in Chicago. Kema smiles as she remembers the phrase Sharon often uses to get inspired to pursue her goals: "Let your haters be your motivators." However, as she continues thinking about the phrase, she decides that it will only provide her short-term motivation because it focuses on proving wrong a group of people who don't like you. There have been "haters" in Kema's life, but she has not focused on them. She views them as a temporary distraction on her way to achieving success.

Kema pulls her car into the garage and as she exits the car, her cellphone begins to ring. It's Wendy. Kema shakes her head and allows the call to go to voicemail. Kema thinks, *Wendy must be feeling guilty about me overhearing her conversation with Lauren. If she leaves a message, I might just delete it without listening to it.*

Once Kema is inside of her condo, her cellphone rings again. She looks at the screen and breathes a sigh of relief when she sees that it's Linda calling her.

"Hello, Kema. Did I call you at a bad time?"

"No, I just arrived home from the office for the last time. I just resigned."

"How do you feel about it?"

"I made the right choice and I'm looking forward to the future."

"That's great to hear. I spoke with Victor to arrange the

paperwork for the purchase agreement. He referred me to Bradley Davis, one of his colleagues at his law firm. I spoke with Mr. Davis and he said we can come to his office on Monday at 2:00 p.m. to sign the paperwork. Are you available?"

"Yes."

"Great, he said that once we get to the building, he will meet us in the lobby and escort us to his office."

"Okay, I'll meet you fifteen minutes before."

Kema ends the call and notices that Wendy has left a voicemail. She lets curiosity prevail and listens to it:

"Hi Kema, this is Wendy. I heard that you resigned from the company. As your mentor, I wish you would have spoken to me first before you made your decision. If you need a reference for another position, I'll be happy to provide one for you. I hope to speak with you soon, take care."

Kema thinks, *unbelievable. Does she think I'm deaf? She knows I overheard her in the elevator. And she is the last person on earth I would contact for a reference.*

Kema puts the phone on her coffee table. It's caused enough excitement for the day.

*

Monday and Kema arrives for the pre-arranged meeting

Please Lord, don't let me see Victor while I'm here, Kema says a quick prayer as she parks her car in the building garage of the law firm. She enters the lobby and sees Linda with her salt-and-pepper hair cascading past her shoulders, dressed in a black and white trimmed suit, and seated in a plush blue chair.

"Good afternoon, Linda. You really dressed up for this. You look nice."

"Hello Kema. This is a special occasion. I'm thankful that you are taking over the store. I can now retire and enjoy more time with my family."

Kema smiles and says, "I'm glad. You've been stressed the past couple of months."

"Yes, I have. Thanks to you, not anymore!"

Before Kema can respond, a rather short, brown-haired man wearing an ill-fitting gray suit approaches them.

"Ms. Pérez and Ms. Daniels?"

"Yes?" Kema and Linda reply in unison.

"Hello, I'm Bradley Davis. I will be facilitating the purchase agreement paperwork. Please follow me to my office."

There, Bradley explains the purchase agreement to them for about ten minutes before they sign it. They both shake hands with him and he walks with them back to the lobby. Before Kema has a chance to say good-bye to Linda, they see Victor walking in the building laughing with a woman who looks familiar to Kema.

"Hello, Victor!" Linda calls out to him. Victor and the woman stop and walk towards them. Kema's request to God to not see Victor had not been honored; she wishes that she were invisible.

"Hello, Ms. Pérez and Ms. Daniels. Have you signed the purchasing agreement?"

Linda replies, "Yes. Thank you for recommending Mr. Davis."

"It was my pleasure. Oh, forgive me for being rude. This is, Griselle Moreno."

"Hello, it's nice to meet you both," Griselle says with a smile.

"It's been good seeing you both, take care," Victor replies as he and Griselle walk swiftly to the elevator.

Kema thinks, *Victor hasn't addressed me formally since the first day we met. I guess he no longer has feelings for me. Victor and Griselle seem to enjoy each other's company, though. Griselle. Why does her name and face seem so familiar?* Kema's thoughts are interrupted by Linda.

"Kema, I think you have all that you need to take over the store. Feel free to contact me any time you have any questions."

*

Kema exits the building and walks to the parking garage.

Thoughts are swirling around in her head about how she is going to manage the store and possibly hire a new employee now that Linda will not be involved in the day-to-day operations of the store. She opens her car door, sits down in the driver's seat, and before she starts the car, Kema suddenly realizes where she has seen Griselle: Griselle is the salsa dance instructor who gave her and Victor a salsa lesson.

Kema grips the steering wheel with both hands and thinks, *wow. He's been in a relationship with Griselle all along. I'm glad that I dismissed him from my life. Good riddance. Time to focus on running this business.* Kema starts the car and drives home to pick up her laptop and drives to Sweet Daddy's Fashions.

CHAPTER 14

Once Kema arrives at the store, she sees Darron at the cash register assisting a customer with a purchase. Kema smiles and greets Darron and the customer as she walks to the back of the store where the office is located. He looks puzzled to see her at the store this early in the afternoon. Kema pulls out her personal laptop and starts revising the business plan for Sweet Daddy's Fashions that was included in the purchasing agreement. Since Christmas is coming, she sets sales goals for November and December along with a holiday marketing campaign. Kema figures that Darron can help her with social marketing to promote the holiday sales. She will discuss the business plan with him after the store closes in three hours. Kema is counting on Darron not having any plans after work. After Darron finishes with the customer, he walks to the office.

"Ms. Kema, I didn't think you were coming into the store today. Is everything okay?"

"Everything's great. I don't know if Ms. Linda told you that I am now the full owner of the store?"

Darron looks confused and replies, "Well, she has been looking happier this week than I have seen her in a while. Especially today when she was heading to an appointment."

"Actually, the appointment was to sign the purchasing agreement that gives me full ownership of the store."

"Oh wow. That explains a lot ... What about your job? I know you're Superwoman, but how can you run the business full-time and maintain your career?"

"I resigned from Resilient Financial. I'm going to give this business all my attention."

"I think Mr. Daniels would be proud that you've taken over."

"I hope I will make him proud. I made a few edits to the store's business plan and I'd like to get your input. Do you have time to discuss it after the store closes? It will only take an hour."

"I have plans to grab food and then meet up with my Principles of Accounting study group at eight."

"Okay, how about I order some food for us and we have a thirty-minute meeting instead?"

"Only if you order ribs, greens, macaroni and cheese, and cornbread from Lonnie's BBQ?"

Kema laughs and says, "How can you eat all that food and still be alert?"

"Easy. All I have to do is walk these cold, windy Chicago streets to meet my study group at a coffee shop. I'll buy a cup of coffee and be ready to study."

Kema orders the food and it is delivered right before she secures the doors to close the store. Kema and Darron eat and discuss the business plan. Kema tells Darron that now that Linda has departed he will assume more responsibilities as an assistant manager. The responsibilities will include interviewing and training new employees and assisting with the holiday season marketing strategy. She asks him to ask if any of his friends are interested in a part-time position in the store. Kema tells Darron that he will receive a bonus in January for assuming the additional duties and that they can negotiate a raise in February. Darron is excited about the new responsibilities and as they leave the store for the night, Kema notices that Darron appears taller and has more swagger in his stride.

*

Kema arrives home and feels sluggish after all of the food she ate with Darron. She'll need to stay awake for a while to allow the food to digest. Kema decides to call her best friend.

"Hey Sharon! How are you doing?"

"Girl, I'm tired. I just came home from a meeting with my stylists at Gracious Cuts III. I'm trying to train them to use an online appointment booking systems to keep our clients organized."

"An online appointment booking system sounds like a great idea. I may need to get your advice on business optimization solutions."

"Hold on … Kema. What are you trying to tell me? Are you a full-time business owner now?"

Kema takes a dramatic pause before she answers. "Yes!"

"Oh Kema. I'm so proud of you! You can ask me for advice anytime. Have you told Ms. Janice?"

"No. I'm bracing myself now for her reaction."

Sharon chuckles and says, "You may need a strong drink before you do."

"You might be right. Please, say a prayer for me. While I have you on the phone, do you know of anyone who is looking for part-time employment during the holiday season?"

"My niece Cassandra, who attends the University of Wisconsin-Madison, will be back in Chicago the first week in December. She is always looking to make extra money to support her shopping habit. I let her work in my shop last Christmas as a receptionist but we clashed because she's noisy and a know-it-all just like my sister Savannah. I didn't have the patience to keep answering her questions and constantly explain my decisions to her. She's a hard worker and is on the Dean's List. I think your personality is a better fit for her than mine. "

"I look forward to speaking with her about working in the store."

"Girl, let me get off this phone and relax. I'll tell Cassandra to send her resume to you."

Kema feels satisfied about her first day as a "boss". With Darron and Sharon's help scouting potential employees, she feels confident that she will have a good team. Kema plans to arrive at the shop each day by seven. This will give her enough time to check email, review the inventory reports, answer customer queries, and restock the store before it opens at ten. Darron arrives at nine and will be able to assist her with the tasks.

Now that Kema has worked out her daily morning agenda, she is ready for bed. She can't help but think that her nights of going to bed before midnight are numbered. Although she plans to leave the store shortly after the store closes at 7:00 p.m., Kema knows that she will be evaluating sales figures and developing marketing strategies once she gets home. To focus on her new responsibilities, she decides that she shouldn't procrastinate about telling Janice about her ownership status.

Kema thinks, *after I close the store, I'll stop by her place with a buttermilk pound cake from Honey Bear Bakery. Mama can't scream loud with her favorite cake in her mouth.*

CHAPTER 15

After closing the store, Kema heads to pick up the buttermilk pound cake that she pre-ordered. Once Kema secures the cake in the backseat of her car, she calls Janice to let her know that she will be stopping by in twenty minutes for a visit. Kema didn't inform Janice about her visit the night before because she knows how she likes to cook for her when she comes to visit. Kema thinks that this will be a quick visit. She doesn't want Janice to make a fuss by preparing a meal specifically for her. Kema figures Janice will do enough fussing when she breaks the news to her about Sweet Daddy's Fashions.

Kema parks the car and opens the backdoor to retrieve the cake. She holds it carefully as if she were holding an infant. When Janice opens the door, she greets Kema with a kiss on the cheek.

"Hey baby! You brought a cake from Honey Bear Bakery! What are we celebrating? Are you now the CEO of Resilient Financial?"

Kema laughs nervously and replies, "No, Mama. If Mr. Reynolds stepped down, there are plenty of people more senior than me to take his place."

"You could be CEO. With God's intervention, nothing is impossible."

"You're right … Do you have any ice cream to go with this cake?"

"I have some butter pecan ice cream in the freezer that's been calling my name for a while. Tonight's the night!"

Kema and Janice indulge in two scoops of ice cream each

to accompany the hearty slices of buttermilk pound cake.

Janice licks the last bite of ice cream from the spoon and says, "The last time you were here, you were stressed about your job. How are you doing now in your new position?"

The moment of truth has arrived and Kema looks Janice in her eyes and replies, "I decided to resign from Resilient Financial and assume full ownership of the store."

"Oh Lord, Kema. You've given up a good paying job to take over your Daddy's little store. Have you lost your mind?"

"No. I haven't lost my mind. You told me to think long and hard about my decision and I did."

"Well, I can't get my blood pressure up over this. The deed is done. It is your life … I will pray for you and put you in God's hands."

"Thank you, Mama. God's hands will uphold me."

"Don't get smart now."

"I'm not getting smart or sassy Mama. I prayed about my decision and I am at peace with it."

"I should have known that you'd already made up your mind. Now I know why you brought this cake over here. You're going to have me stress eating this cake thinking about this. Cut me three more slices of it and you can take the rest home with you. "

"You placed me in God's hands, remember …"

"Hush child and cut the cake."

Kema cut the three slices of cake as instructed and places the rest of the cake in the cake box.

Kema gets up from the kitchen table, kisses Janice on the forehead and says: "I'm leaving now. I have an early day tomorrow. I love you Mama."

"I love you, too. You know I only want the best for you."

"Yes, I know. Don't worry about me. Everything will work out."

*

The next morning Kema arrives at Sweet Daddy's Fashions at seven as she had planned. On Wednesdays, the merchandise delivery truck usually arrives between 7:30 and 8:00 a.m. To her surprise, it is already parked with hazard lights flashing in front of the store. As she walks closer to the truck, she notices that there are two men inside. She looks in through the driver's side window and sees him glaring at her. The passenger, a tall, thin man wearing glasses that are resting on the tip of his nose, gets out the truck and says in a rough tone, "Can you accept the delivery?"

"Yes, I wasn't expecting the delivery truck for another half hour."

"Sometimes our route changes and we get here earlier than 7:30."

"I hope you weren't waiting too long."

"We have been out here for about twenty minutes. Usually, an older lady is always here to sign for the delivery and an older guy helping her. Where are they?"

"She's retired. The older guy was my father. He passed away. I'm now the owner of the store. My name is Kema Daniels. What's your name?"

The man shakes his head in disbelief and replies, "Ma'am I'm sorry for your loss. My name is Patrick Beasley. Everyone calls me Peanut Butter or P.B. for short. I'm looking for a lady to be my Jelly so we can be called P.B. & J."

Kema tries to prevent herself from cackling. She musters the simple reply, "Nice to meet you P.B."

P.B. hands her the delivery slip to sign and helps her load the inventory into the store. As P.B. exits the store, the driver yells, "Come on man, we gonna be late."

P.B. looks back at Kema, waves as he says, "Have a good day, Ms. Kema."

Kema places her left hand on the top of her head and thinks, *I need to arrive at the store on Wednesdays no later than 6:15 a.m. I can't depend on P.B.'s kindness every Wednesday. I may need to hire someone to help me with these deliveries.*

Darron arrives at nine and takes over the inventory stocking. Kema goes into the office and checks her email. She opens an email from Cassandra, Sharon's niece. The email contains a greeting and her attached resume. Kema opens the resume and quickly evaluates it; she is impressed. Cassandra is majoring in retailing and consumer behavior at the University of Wisconsin-Madison. She is the Student Body Government Association vice-president, treasurer for the Marketing Club, and volunteers with Habitat for Humanity. Kema sends Cassandra an email requesting a phone interview with her as soon as possible. Kema leaves the office to ask Darron if his friends expressed interest in working at the store.

"Darron, did you have any luck getting us any job candidates?"

"So far, I haven't had any luck, my friends at school already have part-time jobs or are busy with schoolwork and other activities. I do have a few friends who are not in college that I have not asked."

"No worries. I think I may have a good candidate for the part-time retail position. However, ask your friends who aren't in college if they would be interested in unloading the delivery truck on Wednesdays."

"Sure, I will ask them."

Kema and Darron assist a few customers when the store opens at ten. During the day, the busiest hours are between eleven and two and from four to seven in the evening. Darron usually takes his lunch break at 2:30 p.m. and studies for his classes. Kema decides to take her lunch break at 3:30 p.m. before the store gets busy at four. She remembers that she didn't pack a lunch today and orders a Caesar chicken salad from an Italian restaurant a few blocks away from the store. Although she orders the salad at three, it doesn't arrive until almost four. Kema wolfs down a few bites of her salad in the office before she stores it in the mini refrigerator.

The customers come in steadily until the store closes. Kema locks the door after Darron leaves and returns to the office to eat the rest of the salad before starting on paperwork. She takes the salad out of the refrigerator and before she digs in, she notices the salad has taken on a different form. The lettuce is wilted and the croutons are soggy from the Caesar dressing. Kema shakes her head in disappointment and only eats the chicken. Kema thinks, *salads are off the menu for lunch.*

Kema checks her inbox. Cassandra is available tomorrow at 9:00 a.m. Kema replies to her email with the teleconference number. Now that Kema has scheduled the interview, she reviews the receipts to determine if the sales goal for today has been met. The sales goal was $2000 and the store sold $1300 worth of merchandise – missing the goal by 35%. Kema is not troubled by it because she expects the store traffic to pick up in a few days due to Halloween and the first of the month.

Kema finishes the paperwork around 7:15 p.m. and as she prepares to leave the store, she realizes that she has never interviewed anyone for a position. She walks back to the office with her laptop and searches online for interview questions for a retail sales position. Kema finds a set of questions, copies and pastes them into another document, and saves them in a folder on her laptop labeled "Part-time retail position". Feeling at ease, she finally leaves the store for the night.

CHAPTER 16

Kema arrives at the store the next morning more prepared than she was the previous day. She has packed a lunch of carrots, celery, hummus and a tuna salad sandwich. Kema figures she can snack on the carrots, celery and hummus throughout the day if she can't take a longer break to eat the tuna salad sandwich. The small interior office that she works in now is a far cry from her Resilient Financial office with a lakefront view. Kema snaps herself out of glamorizing her time at the company and reminds herself that they took her office away and told her to earn it again in her new position. Now that she is a leader of her own company, she vows to never treat her staff the way she was treated.

Kema plans for the interview with Cassandra to last for thirty minutes. Ten minutes before the call, Kema attempts to open the folder on the laptop to access the interview questions. To her dismay, the folder does not open. She tries five more times to no avail. Kema thinks, *what is going on? I know I should have printed the questions just in case of technical difficulties. Breathe. I will have to improvise.* Kema dials into the teleconference five minutes before the call and is told by the automated system that Cassandra has already joined.

Kema is already impressed with Cassandra's promptness and begins the interview by giving her background information about the company. In addition, Kema provides an overview of the position duties. She then asks Cassandra to talk about why she is interested in the position. Cassandra replies that it aligns with her major and she hopes her experience working at the store could be used when she writes her senior thesis in two years. She states that on a personal note, she would like to work in the store because she would be contributing to a family legacy. Kema thinks, *I like her enthusiasm and initiative. Did Sharon coach this girl?*

Kema asks Cassandra if she has any questions. Cassandra is very inquisitive and asks about employee training, internship opportunities and workplace culture. Kema answers her questions. However, she knows she will have to explore how an internship program would work with Darron's guidance since he is an informal intern. As Cassandra is articulate and asked thought-provoking questions during the interview, Kema is convinced that she will be an asset to the business and asks if she can start work the first Saturday in December. Cassandra agrees to the start date and Kema emails her paperwork to complete before her first day of work.

Kema emerges from the office with a gigantic smile feeling satisfied that she has hired her first employee. She shares the news with Darron and he is excited about training a new employee to relieve him of some of his duties. Darron tells Kema that his friend, Antonio, is interested in assisting with unloading the delivery truck on Wednesdays and provides Kema with his cell phone number. Kema goes to the office to call him. When he answers the phone, Kema hears blaring music in the background.

"Hello, may I speak to Antonio please?"

"This is him."

"My name is Kema Daniels. Darron gave me your cell phone number. He told me that you're interested in unloading the delivery truck here at Sweet Daddy's Fashions. Can you come to the store tomorrow at 9:30 a.m. for an interview?"

"Yeah, I can be there."

"Okay. I will see you tomorrow morning at 9:30."

"Yup."

Kema hangs up the phone and is uncertain about Antonio. His lackadaisical tone over the phone is not endearing him to her. Fortunately, he will not have to interact with any customers while unloading the delivery truck. Kema may be biased against him since he is not as articulate as Cassandra. Perhaps his tone was not pleasing because she called him at an awkward time. Tomorrow she will know if her intuition about him is true.

*

When Kema arrives at the store, she rearranges the furniture in the office for the interview. Kema moves her desk closer to the wall and places her desk chair in front of the desk, a chair next to her desk chair, and another chair in front of the two chairs forming a triangle. She remembers when she first interviewed for her job at Resilient Financial and how intimidating it was having a person staring at you from behind a desk and judging your every move. Kema does not want to recreate that same interview environment.

Darron arrives at the store at nine. Kema asks Darron if he will interview Antonio with her. He agrees and they sit in her office and review the interview questions that Kema prepared. Five minutes before 9:30, the bell chimes on the store door and Kema looks at the security app on her phone. The app shows a young man standing about five foot ten wearing a black hooded sweater, red ball cap and slim-fit jeans. She hands her phone to Darron.

"Darron, is this Antonio?"

"Yes, that's him."

Kema is relieved that he is on time yet somewhat disappointed that Antonio chose casual attire for a job interview. She and Darron walk to the front of the store and let Antonio inside.

Kema, Darron and Antonio walk into the office. Kema tells Antonio to sit on the first chair. Kema and Darron sit on the chairs in front of the desk.

Kema starts. "Antonio, do you have any experience unloading delivering trucks?"

"Yes"

"Can you tell me about it?"

"On Mondays, Tuesdays, Fridays and Saturdays, I unload delivery trucks at four different stores through a staffing agency. I have been doing it for seven months now. I have been trying to pick up an additional day but the staffing agency can only give me four days of work. My lady is about to have our son in March and diapers are not cheap. When Darron called me and said that you needed some help on Wednesdays, I thought it would be a good look."

Kema looks at Antonio with a puzzled expression on her face and asks: "Can you explain what you mean by 'a good look'?"

"I mean, both of us could benefit. I could use a few extra dollars to help take care of my family and you need someone to unload the truck. It's a win-win situation, you know what I mean?"

"Now, I know what you mean."

Darron asks the next question. "You know how I started working here with Mr. Daniels four years ago and now I have moved up to assistant manager. Can you tell us how working at Sweet Daddy's Fashions will help you with your future goals?"

Antonio takes a deep breath and looks up at the ceiling as if he were summoning strength to answer the question. "My first goal is to be able to provide for my son. My second goal is to save up money to start my associate's degree in information technology. Earning extra money from this job will help with these goals."

Kema is impressed with his response and thinks, *although Antonio is a little rough around the edges, he knows what he wants to do with his life ...*

Kema asks the last question. "I know that Darron recommended you for this job. Can you provide me with another reference?"

"Yes. I can ask Mrs. Claybourne. She is the staffing agency manager who hooked me up ... I'm sorry ... who helped me get the contract unloading trucks at the other stores."

"Great. Once you provide me with her information, we

can get back to you with our decision. Do you have any questions for us?"

"With the holidays coming up, do you think that you'll need someone to do any other jobs around the store?"

"We have already hired one person to assist us with the holiday sales rush. Depending on the traffic inside the store, we may need additional assistance. Do you have any experience working in a retail store?"

"No, but I was thinking that I could help clean the store after it closes or maybe help put the clothes out on display after I unload them."

"Thank you for letting me know your interest. We will keep you in mind if the need arises."

Kema suddenly realizes that in the rush of handling the day-to-day activities of the store, that she forgot to order business cards. Kema reaches for a sticky note and pen on her desk and quickly jots down the store's email address and business cell number. She hands the sticky note to Antonio and says, "You can email or text Mrs. Claybourne's contact information."

Antonio takes the note, folds it, and places it in his jeans pocket and says, "Thank you, Ms. Daniels." He then turns to Darron and gives him a soul handshake before he exits the store.

CHAPTER 17

Fridays are usually busy for Sweet Daddy's Fashions but this Friday is extremely busy. It is the first Friday in November. Twenty minutes after Antonio left the store, the store has been swarming with customers. She and Darron assist customers up until three – an hour past the normal rush. Kema thinks, *I am exhausted. I may need to hire someone specifically for Fridays and perhaps a few hours on Saturdays. I have to check the sales for today and this time last year to justify hiring another person.*

Kema retreats to her office for a quick break. She checks the business email and sees that Antonio has provided Mrs. Claybourne's email and phone number. Kema is pleasantly surprised by Antonio's promptness and proceeds to send Mrs. Claybourne an email requesting a date and time for a brief conversation about Antonio's work history. After Kema sends the email, she pulls out a sandwich bag of cashews from her lunch bag and begins to eat them. As soon as she gets up from her desk chair to throw the bag away, she hears a "ding" from the laptop letting her know that a new email is in the inbox. It's Mrs. Claybourne confirming her availability for a call.

*

On Monday morning, Kema calls Mrs. Claybourne.

"Hello, Samantha Claybourne speaking."

"Hello, Mrs. Claybourne. This is Kema Daniels."

"Can you tell me about your experience working with Antonio?"

"I have worked with Antonio for about seven months.

However, I've known him for a year. Antonio is persistent. He called and came to the staffing agency every day checking to see if I had any positions. I haven't received any complaints about Antonio arriving to the job sites late or behaving rudely. I know he is a hard worker because he constantly asks about picking up an extra day at another job site, but we don't have anything right now."

Kema sits back in her chair, smiles, and replies: "Thank you, Mrs. Claybourne for giving me insight on Antonio's work ethic.

Kema ends the call and thinks, *I should call Antonio now and tell him he has the job. Hopefully I will hear some enthusiasm in his voice after I tell him.*

Kema dials his number and he answers after the third ring.

"Hello?"

"Hi, Antonio. This is Kema Daniels. How are you?

"I'm good."

"I spoke with Mrs. Claybourne and she spoke really highly of you. Can you start unloading the delivery truck this Wednesday?"

Antonio pauses before he replies, "Yes, I can. What time should I get to the store?"

"Please arrive at the store at 6:45 a.m."

"Okay. I will be there. Thank you, Ms. Daniels."

"Thank you, Antonio. I will see you on Wednesday at 6:45."

Kema ends the call and thinks: *He did sound more enthusiastic this time than the last conversation. I think he will be a great addition to our team.*

*

Since Daylight Saving Time has ended, the days are short and the nights are long. Kema arrives at the store on Wednesday morning at 6:15. Kema feels that she is in constant darkness; it's dark when she arrives to the store and when she leaves. Janice worries about her opening and closing the store by herself. To alleviate her fears, she texts her when she arrives at the store, leaves the store, and when she arrives home. All the checking-in adds to Kema's long list of responsibilities; however, she is grateful that someone is concerned about her well-being.

After texting Janice, Kema checks the business email inbox and creates a personnel folder for Antonio on the laptop. She imagines the day when she will have someone managing the day-to-day operations of Sweet Daddy's Fashions and she can concentrate on making strategic decisions. Being a visionary for the business is her goal. Before she can daydream further, she looks up at the security camera and sees that Antonio is outside. Kema walks to the front of the store to let him in.

"Good morning, Antonio."

"Good morning," Antonio replies, appearing to be battling tiredness.

"The truck hasn't arrived yet. I asked you to arrive a little early because it can arrive much earlier than the 7:30 a.m. scheduled arrival. On my first day, the truck arrived twenty minutes early."

"What time do you usually get to the store?"

"I usually get to the store at seven each morning."

"Do you usually open the store by yourself every day?"

Kema is unsure how she wants to answer the question. He hasn't completed his first day yet and he is asking about how she opens the store. Kema thinks, *well, he knows now that I open the store by myself.*

"Today, I had to make sure I was here to give you a brief orientation before you start."

"Okay. Let me know if you need me to arrive when you get here on Wednesday."

"I wouldn't want to inconvenience you by asking you to arrive much earlier."

"I know I wouldn't want my mom or any of my female family members to be by themselves this early in this neighborhood."

Kema gives Antonio a quick tour of the store before the truck arrives at 7:40 a.m. Kema and Antonio go outside. P.B. recognizes Kema from the last delivery and hops out the truck to greet her.

"Good morning, Ms. Kema! Do you need me to help you unload today?"

"Good morning, P.B. Let me introduce you to Antonio who'll be doing that."

P.B. looks at Antonio skeptically and says: "What's up young blood?"

Antonio replies blankly, "Nothing, but the sky."

Kema is confused by this interaction and attempts to break the tension. "It's too cold out here for me. I'll leave you gentlemen to your work. Antonio, stop in the office once you finish unloading."

Antonio replies without breaking eye contact with P.B. "I will.

Kema returns to her office and reviews the new inventory spreadsheet trying not to monitor the outdoor security camera, which might explain the tension between the two men.

Antonio comes into Kema's office after an hour and announces that he is finished. Kema shows him how to unpack the boxes and fold the clothes to place on the display shelves. Before she shows him how to hang clothes on the rack, Darron arrives and begins training him.

Antonio works three hours his first day. Kema pays him a flat fee of $100 for unloading the truck and an extra $30 for assisting with unpacking and arranging the merchandise. She thinks the investment in Antonio is worth it because it gets her closer to focusing on other aspects of the business.

*

The next week, Kema takes Antonio up on his offer to arrive at the store at 6:15 on Wednesdays. She wakes up a little earlier to purchase coffee and half a dozen donuts at Doughman's Donuts two blocks away from the store. Kema doesn't know if Antonio is a coffee drinker; however, she assumes that if he doesn't like coffee, he can eat donuts. Kema packed some chai tea from home in a thermal container, a change from her usual morning herbal tea. She plans to treat herself to a donut and leave the rest for Antonio and Darron.

Kema turns the engine off on her car and sips tea while she waits for Antonio to arrive at the front of the store. Before she takes her second sip, she sees him sprinting towards the store as if he were trying to escape the grip of the cold wind. Kema gets out the car with the coffee and donuts, greets Antonio, and opens the store.

"Good morning, Antonio. Thank you for meeting me early. I have coffee and donuts!"

"Thank you. I didn't have time to get a cup of coffee. I usually skip breakfast, but I may eat a donut before I leave today."

"Make sure you pick out your favorite donut before Darron gets here. He loves them."

Antonio chuckles as he looks in the donut box and says, "You're right. Darron goes hard on food. He eats the most out of all of my friends."

Kema laughs along with him and then thinks about whether she should ask Antonio about the tension he had with P.B. the previous week. She thinks, *I want to know, but I don't want to make him feel uncomfortable. On the other hand, I don't want this situation to get out of control. If P.B. is initiating hostility I should inform whoever he reports to.*

"Antonio, I noticed that you and P.B. weren't friendly towards one another. Do you have an issue with him or vice versa?"

Antonio looks down at his shoes and then directly in Kema's eyes and replies, "That old man is a hater. He lives in my building on the same floor as me and my lady Natalie. But he's been trying to get with her, telling her he can treat her better, treat her right. He talks trash about me and he doesn't even know me."

Kema is taken aback. P.B. seemed so thoughtful. She

would have never guessed that he would behave in that way. On second thought, she could believe it. Kema remembers how charming Victor was until he displayed his opportunistic side.

Kema replies, "That's unfortunate that P.B. disrespected you and your girlfriend. I don't want him to create a hostile environment for you. Did you all exchange words while you were unloading the truck?"

"No. He sat back in the cab after he opened the back of the truck. I tried not to look at him afterwards. He probably didn't want to show out in front of the truck driver. That man looks like he doesn't play games."

Kema laughs and says, "I agree. I thought he was going to reprimand *me* for arriving late on my first day signing for the delivery."

The delivery truck arrives at the scheduled time. Kema and Antonio walk outside. Kema notices that P.B. is not in the passenger side of the truck. *Maybe he took the day off or stopped working for the trucking company.* She does not feel courageous enough to ask the truck driver about P.B. and she knows that Antonio could care less.

The driver turns off the vehicle and grunts a greeting as he exits his side and walks past Kema and Antonio to open the back. He hands Kema a clipboard containing the form to sign for the delivery. As she returns the clipboard back to him, she quickly asks, "Where is P.B. today?"

The driver looks at Kema and says, "He was a no-show today and I couldn't find a replacement. Now I'm stuck doing this route by myself."

"I hope the day isn't too rough for you."

"Hope is all that I have now. I hope it is enough to get me through."

Kema thinks fast and replies, "I need to go into the store quickly. Can you hold on for one minute?"

"Only for one minute."

Kema retrieves the box of donuts and some napkins and heads back out to the truck. She holds out the box to the driver.

"Would you like a donut?"

A broad smile comes across the truck driver's face as he reaches for a napkin to retrieve a donut. *Who would have thought that a donut would turn his frown into a smile?*

"Thank you, Ms.," he says.

"You are welcome. I'm Kema by the way."

"Thank you, Ms. Kema. My name is Joseph."

CHAPTER 18

December 2019

It's the first week of December and the holiday season has begun. During this busy time, Kema has created a uniform consisting of long-sleeved polo shirts, black slacks and black shoes, which is a drastic change from her stylish clothes she used to wear at Resilient Financial. Cassandra begins working in the store on Friday, December 6th. Kema slept only three hours a night the previous week preparing the employee manual, which she has revised at least ten times. Darron offered to assist her with it. However, she didn't want to burden him with this task because of his long hours at the store and his schoolwork.

On Friday, Kema arrives at the store at eight instead of seven. Yawning her way inside the store's entrance with a thermos filled with green tea in her right hand and her laptop bag on her left shoulder, she trips over her feet and falls to the floor. Somehow, she manages to keep the thermos in her hand after the fall; however, the laptop bag is now in front of the shoe display – about four feet away from the front door.

Kema closes her eyes and thinks, *please let this not be an indication of how this day is going to go.* She slowly gets off the floor and feels pain in her knees as she hobbles to the shoe display to retrieve the laptop bag. Once she's in the office, she pulls out her cellphone from her purse and sees three texts and five missed calls from Janice. Kema didn't tell her that she was arriving to the store an hour late today. Kema braces herself for the lecture she will hear from Janice as she returns her call.

"Kema, are you alright? I have been worried sick. I have

been texting and calling for over an hour."

"I'm alright Mama. I woke up late this morning."

"I wish you would have told me you planned to do that. You know there are a lot of crazy things happening in the world."

"Yes, ma'am I apologize."

"You don't sound like you feel well."

"I'm just tired from working late."

"I haven't seen you since you stopped by for Thanksgiving. I know that your only off day is on Sunday and you spend that time for yourself. But you need to take some time out to praise, worship and honor God who gives you the strength to run that store. Can we go to church this Sunday morning?"

Kema knows Janice is right. She hasn't been to church in over a month. However, she thinks that she can take time out in her home for worship and praise and won't have to figure out what to wear to church.

"I can't promise that I'll make it to church on Sunday, but I will come by to see you."

"Okay, baby. Let me know if you change your mind."

Although Kema will be thirty-six years old next August, Janice always manages to make her feel like she is still living under her roof. Kema figures that this is the tax she pays for being an only child – her mother focuses all of her attention on her because she doesn't have any siblings. In addition, Janice doesn't have a significant other to fuss over. The only friends she has are the ladies who attend church with her and all of them are single. About once a month, they get together and go to dinner. In the spring and summer time, they attend church revivals. Kema has asked her mother several times if she would date again, but she just responds that she is happy and content in the state that she is in. Kema knows that Janice is paraphrasing a Bible verse but hasn't taken the time to look it up.

Lost in her thoughts, Kema looks at the security monitor and sees that Darron is coming into the store and leaves her office to meet him.

"Good morning, Darron."

"Hi Ms. Kema. Are you okay? You're limping."

"I tripped and fell as I was walking into the store this morning."

"You should stay seated in your office today. I can train the new lady once she arrives. What time is she coming in?"

"9:30"

Darron rubs his hands together and says, "Alright, she will arrive in thirty minutes' time. Can I look at the employee manual?"

"Oh, I haven't had a chance to print it. Let me do that now."

Kema hobbles back to the office and attempts to print the manual. However, her laptop is not communicating with the printer. She breaks out in a cold sweat and calls out to Darron.

"Darron, can you come to the office?"

Darron tries uploading the latest printer software to the laptop to see if this will rectify the problem. The document still won't print. Darron says, "I wish I'd brought my laptop to see if I could connect it to the printer. Don't panic, I can walk her through the basics of the job and maybe tomorrow we can give her a copy of the employee manual."

Wiping her forehead with a paper napkin, Kema replies: "That's a good plan."

*

The security system beeps to alert that there is motion at the front door. Kema looks at the security monitor and sees a petite woman dressed in a forest green peacoat and black high-heeled boots outside the door. This must be Cassandra. Kema walks to the door to let her in.

"Hello Cassandra, I'm Kema. So nice to meet you."

"Good morning, Ms. Kema. It's great to meet you as well."

"This is Darron, our assistant manager, who will be working closely with you today."

Darron smiles brightly and extends his hand to Cassandra. "Welcome, Cassandra, I'll try to teach you everything I know."

Cassandra smirks as she extends her hand to shake his and replies, "Thank you, I'm looking forward to learning."

Kema says, "If you need me, I'll be in the office."

Kema decides to make a stop in the restroom before she returns to the office. As she washes her hands, she looks in the mirror and notices she has a piece of napkin shaped like an isosceles triangle on her forehead. She makes an aggravated face, plucks it off and thinks, *how embarrassing! Why didn't Darron tell me I had something on my face?*

Kema stays in the office most of the day but comes out periodically unbeknownst to Darron and Cassandra to observe how Darron is training her. Darron is smiling like a Cheshire cat at Cassandra while showing her how to operate the cash register. Cassandra maintains a stoic expression while asking him questions during the training. As the store gets crowded with customers, Darron assists the customers on the floor and to Kema's surprise, Cassandra scans their items at the cash register.

Kema leaves her office to go into the store ten minutes before Cassandra's shift ends to get feedback from her about her first day. Cassandra is standing at the cash register shifting her weight from one foot to the other.

"Hi Cassandra, how did it go?"

"I thought it went well. I see Fridays are very busy. I have one question though?"

"Yes?"

"Can I have a chair to use while I'm ringing up customers' items? My feet are killing me."

Kema stifles a chuckle and replies, "I don't think sitting on a chair when dealing with customers is appropriate. However, I would wear different shoes tomorrow. Those boots you're wearing look stylish but they don't look too comfortable."

"Well, if I can't have a chair. Can you provide an anti-fatigue mat?"

Kema has never heard of an anti-fatigue mat and is amazed that Cassandra knew to ask about this.

"Are you referring to a specific type of mat used for standing?" she asks.

"Yes."

"I should have one available for you to use by next week."

"Okay. Thanks.

Darron chimes in, "Ms. Kema, can we have two mats because usually two employees are behind the checkout counter?"

Kema didn't think she would have this additional expense and tries not to sound agitated when she replies, "Thank you for reminding me. I'll buy two mats. Well, look at the time. I don't want to keep you past your shift, Cassandra."

"I can work overtime if needed."

"I'll keep that in mind as the holiday season progresses. See you tomorrow, Cassandra."

Cassandra replies as she walks gingerly towards the door: "I'll see you tomorrow."

Kema watches Cassandra exit and waits about a minute afterwards to talk to Darron.

CHAPTER 19

"Darron, how did the training go?"

"I think it went well. Cassandra asks a lot of questions, but she learns quickly."

"Good to hear. I troubleshooted the laptop communication with the printer and discovered that the store's Wi-Fi instability was preventing us from printing the employee manual. When the Wi-Fi started working this afternoon, I printed it."

"Okay, Ms. Kema. I see you have skills!"

"Thanks! I can email the employee manual to you tonight and we can place the printed manual behind the counter for you and Cassandra to review tomorrow morning. Will you have time to look at it yourself by then?"

"Sure."

After the store closes, Kema and Darron leave the store at the same time. Kema decides to go to an office supply warehouse store to purchase the anti-fatigue mats. Kema purchases the mats for $40 each and is relieved that they weren't too expensive.

Saturday is another busy day at the store and Kema arrives at her normal time and places the mats behind the counter. When Darron arrives, he's elated to see them and struts on the mats like a rooster. Once Cassandra arrives, she evaluates the mats and then asks, "Ms. Kema, do you know the thickness of these mats? The best mats for standing for long periods have a three-quarter inch thickness."

Kema thinks, *this girl has lost her mind if she thinks that I'm going to return these mats if they don't meet her thickness require-*

ments. Kema takes a deep breath and replies, "I'm not sure of the thickness, but I am sure that the mats will be more comfortable than standing on the concrete floor."

Cassandra walks across one of the mats with her black flats and says, "I guess this will work."

It takes all the strength Kema can muster to prevent her from giving Cassandra a dirty look. "I'm glad that you approve. Darron will go over the employee manual with you today. I'll be in my office if you have any questions."

Kema is exhausted from reviewing paperwork all day and decides to check in with her staff five minutes before Cassandra's shift ends.

"Hello team, how did it go today?"

Darron opens his mouth to reply but Cassandra interjects: "Darron told me I can take breaks throughout the day, but the employee manual doesn't contain any information on the length of the breaks. Also, there is no section on workplace culture or internship opportunities as we discussed during my interview."

"Okay, noted. In the next revision, I'll include it. As far as internship opportunities, I think this should be addressed in another document that Darron and I will draft."

"I can contribute to the workplace culture segment before my seasonal employment ends."

"That will be much appreciated."

"Do you know when you and Darron will draft the internship opportunities document?"

"Once we finish with the holiday season, Darron and I will set up a time to discuss it."

"I also noticed that you came out to check on us later than you did yesterday. Do you think we can schedule team meetings before and after our shifts to discuss issues?"

"That's a great idea. We can implement team meetings starting on Monday."

*

Kema sleeps late and misses Sunday morning service with her mother. She wakes up and sees missed calls and text messages from Janice. She texts Janice back telling her that she will stop by in the afternoon. Knowing that she is long overdue for a spiritual message, she turns on her television to the channel listings. Kema has a "bedside church service" by watching Bishop Franklin Grant, a televangelist on the Abba Father Gospel Channel.

Bishop Grant's message is on maintaining your joy and peace when others try your patience. He suggests extending grace to those who aggravate you because God extends grace to us when we do things that do not please Him. Bishop Grant also recommends expressing gratitude through prayer and meditation at the beginning and end of each day as a shield against your mood being affected by others behavior.

Kema shouts at the television, "Prayer and meditation: that's what's missing from my routine!"

After the message, Kema showers, dresses and drives to Janice's home. Although Janice didn't say that she was cooking anything, Kema anticipates the home-cooked meal that Janice has prepared for them. Kema continues her Sunday service by listening to her gospel music playlist in the car on the way to Janice's home. Kema sings along to the gospel song *Order My Steps* and feels God's presence surrounding her and it seems she arrives at Janice's home quicker than usual.

Kema uses her key to open the door and she is astonished to see a pair of men's dress shoes resting outside the coat closet. Kema thinks, *Mama didn't say that we were having a dinner guest. Whose shoes are these?* She hears Janice's laughter followed by a deep laugh from a male voice coming from the kitchen. Kema walks into the kitchen and startles Janice who is sitting at the table across from a man.

"Kema! I didn't hear you coming through the door. Deacon Julius, this is my daughter Kema."

The man stands up and extends his hand to Kema. "Hello,

Ms. Kema. I'm Julius Chambers. It's a pleasure to meet you. Your mother has told me so much about you."

"Hello, it's nice to meet you."

Janice smiles, bats her eyes at Deacon Julius and says, "I invited Deacon Julius to have dinner with us."

"I couldn't turn down this dinner invitation especially when your mother told me that she was cooking barbeque ribs, macaroni and cheese, turnip greens, candied yams and cornbread. It's like she knew this was my favorite meal."

Janice giggles and playfully slaps Deacon Julius's hand as she rises from the kitchen chair to open the oven. Kema thinks, *what have I walked in on? Mama has makeup and perfume on. She usually only puts on lipstick for church. I've never seen her so enamored with a man before. By the sounds I heard as I was walking in the kitchen, Deacon Julius seems hungry for more than a meal.*

Deacon Julius has an athletic build and stands about five foot eight, with dark brown eyes, and a dark chocolate complexion. His head is shaved and judging from his salt-and-pepper beard, he appears to be in his early sixties.

Janice hasn't prepared a meal like this in a long time. In between bites of food, Kema asks Deacon Julius some questions.

"Deacon Julius, I've never seen you at our church. Where do you attend?"

"Greater Bethel Baptist Church. We are a sister church to yours."

"How did you and Mama meet?"

"I first met your mother five years ago when she and her friends attended a summer revival hosted by my church. The revival that day was packed and people who arrived late had to sit in the deacons' section in the front row. Your mother sat beside me and we shared a hymnal book. Since I arrived early to set up each night for the revival, I made sure I saved four seats for your mother and her friends. On the last day of the revival, I asked if we could keep in touch and she gave me her email address. I emailed her every week to keep in touch and I visit your church once a month on Sundays that I don't have deacon duties at my church. Every time I visit, I teasingly ask your mother when she is going to invite me over for dinner. She would laugh in my face each time! I thought she was kidding with me when she told me to come over for dinner this Sunday until I walked in the kitchen and saw that she had been cooking."

Kema says, "What an interesting story!"

Deacon Julius dabs the corner of his mouth with a napkin, smiles sheepishly as he turns toward Janice and replies, "I hope it won't be my last invitation."

Janice smiles at him and replies, "Next time you're taking *me* out for dinner."

"Sister Janice, I owe you several dinners based on this delicious meal that you prepared. Well, I hate to eat and run but I must get going. I know that you ladies probably have a lot to catch up on."

Deacon Julius rises from the chair, pats his expanded stomach and says, "It was nice to meet you Ms. Kema. Hopefully, I'll see you again. Perhaps at church or when your mother prepares another bountiful spread?"

Kema chuckles and replies, "Yes. Enjoy the rest of your day."

Janice walks Deacon Julius out to the door and Kema resists the temptation to leave the kitchen and look out the living room window to see if Deacon Julius will try to hug or kiss Janice. Kema clears the dishes from the kitchen table and thinks, *Mama's been hiding this man for five years telling me that she didn't want to date, but Deacon Julius clearly has other plans.*

CHAPTER 20

Kema is washing dishes when Janice returns to the kitchen and starts nonchalantly putting the food away. Kema looks at Janice and asks, "Did he give you a kiss goodbye?"

Janice laughs and says, "Stay out of grown folks' business."

"Now I see why you said you didn't want to date. Deacon Julius has been courting you."

"Deacon Julius is my friend. I can't have a friend over for dinner?"

"You don't invite your female church friends over for dinner ..."

"That's because we always go out to dinner when we get together. That's enough talk about me. Let's talk about you. I haven't seen you in weeks and I hardly get to talk to you now that you're a business owner. You know you shouldn't let that business make you so tired that you can't worship the Lord on Sunday. Pastor Wilson gave a powerful sermon on the power of forgiveness and focused on the verse, I think the verse is Mark 11:25, which says every time that you pray you should forgive other people so God can forgive you. This really made me think about your Daddy and how I didn't forgive him for leaving us. I think I blocked some of my blessings and happiness by not forgiving him. I ran right up to the altar during the group prayer part of the service to ask God to forgive me for my unforgiveness."

"It sounds like you had an epiphany during the sermon."

"An apipha what?

"An epiphany is when you suddenly realize something. People on television call it an 'A-ha moment'."

"Yes, that's exactly what it was and I know I can't afford to have any more of my blessings blocked by holding onto grudges."

"I listened to Bishop Franklin Grant on television today and had my own 'A-ha moment' while he was preaching on keeping joy and peace when people are aggravating you. I realized that I need to develop a habit of praying and meditating when I wake up and before I go to sleep. Bishop Grant said doing this will help you deal with others."

"Who's aggravating you at that little store? Is it that college boy trying to act like he's the boss?"

"No, Mama, Darron has been supportive and his responsibilities have increased as a result. I hired a young lady to help during the holiday season. Her name is Cassandra, she's Sharon's niece."

"Why would you hire her? They say it's not a good idea to hire friends or family ..."

"Sharon warned me that Cassandra is inquisitive and opinionated but she assured me that my personality would be able to cope with her quirks. Cassandra has only been working two days and she's already gotten on my nerves."

"You can't let her stress you out. Don't be too meek and mild. Let her know that you're the boss."

"I will."

Kema and Janice finish cleaning the kitchen and settle into the living room to binge watch episodes of the show *Married to Medicine*. Janice is yelling at the characters on the show as if they can hear what she is saying and change their behavior. Kema doesn't know what is more amusing – the show or Janice's reaction to it. She looks at her cellphone and realizes that she hasn't planned for Monday morning. Kema says goodbye to Janice.

When Kema arrives home, she sends a group text to Darron and Cassandra telling them that the first team briefing will be at 9:30. She says she will schedule individual fifteen-minute end-of-shift briefings with each of them to discuss any issues or provide feedback. Kema showers, prays, meditates and falls fast asleep.

*

Kema's morning and end-of-shift meetings with her team are successful. The meetings help Kema to develop a rapport with Cassandra. After the business portion of the end-of-shift meetings with Cassandra, they discuss their love of designer clothes. Kema also tells Cassandra about her time at Resilient Financial and gives her advice on navigating the corporate workplace. Kema allows Cassandra to draft the workplace culture section of the employee manual. Cassandra immediately tells Darron about her latest project and he informs Kema that he will work on an outline for the internship opportunities document for her to review by January.

The week before Christmas, Kema asks Antonio if he can work a full-time shift on Wednesdays and part-time on Friday evenings. He is grateful for the hours and Darron trains him on the cash register while Cassandra assists customers on the storeroom floor. Kema reviews the sales figures and notices that sales this month have exceeded the projected amount by forty percent. After the store closes on Friday, December 20th, Kema gives each team member a Christmas bonus of $500.

Darron says, "Now I can finish my Christmas shopping!"

"I want to use the money to buy a pair of suede knee-high boots, but I'll use it to pay off my credit card bill," Cassandra says.

Antonio is teary-eyed as he says, "Ms. Kema, thank you so much. I really needed the extra money."

"You're welcome, Antonio. You worked hard – all of you worked hard – and the store wouldn't be successful if it wasn't for all of your contributions."

Kema spends Christmas Day with Janice but leaves her home by five so she can rest for the day-after-Christmas rush at the store. The store is swarming with customers as soon as the store opens. Kema is unable to work in her office and has to assist customers at the cash register. Kema doesn't mind helping because the additional sales may allow her to take a small salary from the business. She's been living off her savings and is hoping to take a salary next year.

Kema incorporates Cassandra's workplace culture section in the employee manual a week before she returns to Wisconsin for school. Cassandra now has a product to include in her senior thesis and tells Kema that she looks forward to working with her when she returns to Chicago during spring break.

New Year's Eve has arrived and Kema is reflecting on the events of this year as she reviews the sales figures. What a year it has been! She never would have imagined that all in one year she would have reunited with her father then buried him, gained a promotion and then resigned from her job to take ownership of her father's business, and dated a "good man" and end the relationship. Kema prays a quick prayer to settle her mind.

Lord, thank you for all that you have brought me through this year. I look forward to staying in your presence as you direct my path in 2020.

Noticing that the traffic into the store has slowed, Kema closes the store at four instead of seven to give Darron a break.

As Darron is walking out of the store he turns and says, "Ms. Kema, I hope you're not going to stay here for the rest of the evening and work."

Kema chuckles and replies, "That was my plan, but on second thought, I'll leave with you. Can you wait for a few minutes to let me gather my things?"

"Sure!"

Kema goes to the office to get her purse and hears an alert from her phone. She digs in her purse and pulls out her phone to see a text message from Janice. She's forwarded a digital flyer of a New Year's Eve service at Greater Bethel Baptist Church with the following text message:

Deacon Julius's church is having this service tonight and I will be attending. You should come.

Kema shakes her head and thinks, *I really want to rest tonight, but I do the same thing each New Year's Eve: stay home, write my New Year's resolutions, eat snacks and flip through all the New Year's Eve celebrations on television.* She places her phone back in her purse and walks out to meet Darron who is standing by the door looking at his phone.

"I'm ready now. Do you have plans with your friends this evening?"

Darron looks up from his phone and replies: "Yes, we're hanging out at the arcade in Lincoln Park."

"That sounds like fun. Be safe out there and Happy New Year!"

CHAPTER 21

It never fails. Every time Kema arrives home from work, she feels more fatigued than when she left. Kema is lying across her bed telling herself that she will close her eyes for just a thirty-minute nap. She wakes up two hours later when her phone rings. Kema lifts her weary body from the bed and sees that it is Janice calling her.

"Hello?"

"Hey, baby. You sound like you were asleep. I thought you would still be working."

"Hi Mama. I closed the store early today."

"Good for you. Did you get my message about the service tonight? Deacon Julius is picking me up at 7:30. You can come now and we can ride together or you can meet us at the church. The service starts at eight."

"I didn't realize how tired I am. I think I'll stay home and rest."

"Okay. I'll be praying for you. Happy New Year!"

"Happy New Year, Mama."

Kema hangs up the phone and tries to fall back to sleep. After fifteen minutes of tossing and turning, she gets out of bed and goes to the kitchen to make a turkey sandwich. She devours it and pulls out her New Year's resolution notebook to write down her goals. Kema uses her pen to draw a quadrant on the page. She labels the first quadrant "business goals", the second quadrant "personal development goals", the third quadrant "spiritual goals" and the fourth quadrant "dreamer goals". She places goals in all of the quadrants except "dreamer goals".

Kema has always been practical and results oriented. No one would describe her as a lady with her head stuck in the clouds dreaming and wishing on a star that something would happen. Never one to back away from a challenging situation, Kema writes: *plan a trip to Italy for my birthday*. The thought of traveling excites her. She puts down the notebook and gets out her laptop to search online for Italian destinations. After about an hour, she finds the perfect trip for her. It is a ten-day tour of Italy that includes airfare, accommodation, breakfast and transportation to the cities on the itinerary. The tour starts in Milan with sightseeing in Florence, Venice, the Vatican City and the Amalfi Coast. She looks at the reviews for the trip and all of them are no lower than four out of five stars. Kema doesn't know who could go with her but this doesn't deter her from emailing the travel coordinator to reserve her spot.

Feeling exhaustion kicking in again, Kema takes a shower and goes back to sleep.

*

Because the store was closed New Year's Day, which was on a Wednesday, the delivery truck arrives on Thursday. Antonio tells Kema that he may be able to rearrange his schedule to work on Thursday, however, she gets a text from him early Thursday morning while she was in the donut shop saying that he can't make it. Kema purchases a few extra donuts, hoping that she can entice Joseph to help her unload the truck. When she checked the inventory spreadsheet on New Year's Eve, it didn't look like a large shipment was going to arrive because the holiday sales are over.

When the truck arrives, Kema notices that Joseph is driving and P.B. is back in the passenger seat. Joseph gives Kema a nod to say hello. The truck barely slows to a complete stop before P.B. hops out of the truck.

"Happy New Year, Ms. Kema!"

"Happy New Year, P.B. How are you?"

With a toothy grin P.B. replies, "I'm doing fine now that I

see you."

Kema holds back her laugh and replies, "It's good to see you too. Can you do me a favor?"

"Anything for you ..."

"Antonio couldn't make it today to unload the truck. Do you think you could help me?"

"Young blood stood you up? That sounds about right. I'm pretty sure I can help. But before I get in trouble let me clear it with the boss man." P.B. yells to Joseph, "Aye Joe, can I help Ms. Kema unload the truck?"

Joseph replies, "Sure. I'll help too. Ms. Kema, I could use a donut and maybe a cup of coffee after we finish."

"Man, you can't be asking her for all of that to unload the truck. Where are your manners?"

Kema laughs and replies, "No problem, guys. I came prepared today with coffee and donuts."

Kema signs for the delivery and Joseph and P.B. quickly unload the truck. Kema retrieves the coffee and donuts from the store and gives them to Joseph and P.B.

"Thank you, Ms. Kema. This will get us through the morning," Joseph says.

P.B. turns to Kema and tilts his head and says, "Yeah, thank you, Ms. Kema. You know what else would get me through my morning?"

Kema asks uneasily, "Now, what would that be?"

"A hug."

Without missing a beat Kema replies, "A handshake for all your hard work will be more appropriate don't you think?"

"I really want a hug, but I'll take a handshake for now."

Kema extends her gloved hand and P.B. shakes it but before she is able to release her hand from his grip, he lifts it to his lips and kisses it.

Joseph shoves P.B. and says, "Man, she said a handshake. Give you an inch, and you'll take a mile. I apologize for his behavior. This will not happen again. Let's go P.B."

P.B. winks at Kema and says, "See you next week, Ms.

Kema."

Kema shakes her head as she watches Joseph and P.B. get in the truck and drive away. She walks back into the store and starts unpacking the delivery boxes and placing the merchandise on the display. When Darron arrives, he's surprised to see that she is only half finished.

"Good morning Ms. Kema, where is Antonio today?"

Kema looks up from the boxes and says, "Good morning Darron. Antonio had to work at his other job today. Not many boxes were delivered today and I decided I would unpack so you wouldn't have so much to do when you arrived."

"I appreciate that Ms. Kema. I can take over now."

Kema walks back to the office and reviews the store's gross margin growth from the holidays. The gross margin growth at eight percent exceeded her three percent projection. With this information, Kema decides that she will offer Darron a raise today instead of waiting until February. After the store closes for the day, Kema and Darron agree upon a ten percent raise and Darron presents her with an outline of the internship opportunities document. Kema is impressed but not surprised with Darron's initiative because it validates her decision to give him a raise a month early.

CHAPTER 22

February is usually a slow month for retail in-store clothing sales. However, Sweet Daddy's Fashions sales increased by two percent. This increase is due to Darron being in charge of maintaining the store's e-commerce website and advertising on social media. Sweet Daddy's Fashions Valentine's Day marketing campaign exceeds her expectations in online sales. As a result, a week before Valentines' Day, Kema offers Antonio a full-time position fulfilling orders.

Valentine's Day arrives and it's a sweet day for Kema. She is reviewing the sales figures and calculates that she can take a $2500 salary in March. Grateful that she will not have to use all of her savings on her bills, Kema plans to split the salary four ways by placing $500 each towards her mortgage, savings, investments and vacation. Kema figures that with her leadership, sales will continue to increase and she might be able to start planning to open another retail store in Chicago by fall 2021.

Kema usually doesn't have plans on Valentine's Day, but Janice has a date with Deacon Julius and has asked Kema to come over to help her get ready. Darron agrees to close the store tonight and Kema leaves at five.

Kema arrives to Janice's a half hour later and sees her eyes glued to the national nightly news.

"Mama, aren't you supposed to be getting ready for your date?"

"Hush child. I'm trying to hear about the coronavirus that is spreading across China. They're saying that San Diego is in a public health emergency and people are stuck on a cruise ship because of this virus. Deacon Julius was talking about us taking a cruise but I don't know if I want to do it now."

"Wow, Mama. I liked the way that you casually mentioned a potential trip with Deacon Julius as if it is something you do every day."

Janice doesn't respond and they both watch the news, which also mentions that some experts think that the coronavirus will be seasonal and end when spring arrives. The news finishes and Kema helps Janice select an outfit and do her makeup.

Kema looks through Janice's closet and is dissatisfied with the clothes in the closet. "Mama, I wish you would have told me about your date sooner. We could have shopped for an outfit this weekend."

"Baby, you know you're only available on Sundays and I didn't want to bother you."

"Where are you going tonight?"

"He's taking me to dinner and a movie."

Kema thinks, *good, there won't be many people looking at them at the movies.* She selects a red sequin sweater, black slacks and black flats from Janice's closet.

Janice gets dressed and Kema does her makeup. Janice looks in the mirror and says, "I don't look like myself. Deacon Julius will think he's at the wrong house."

Kema laughs and says, "Mama, you look gorgeous. I'm sure Deacon Julius will recognize you."

The doorbell rings and Kema opens the door for Deacon Julius who is carrying a dozen red roses. He is dressed in a black fedora hat, black suit and a red sequin tie.

"Hello, Deacon Julius. Come on in."

"Hello Ms. Kema. Is Janice ready?"

Before Kema can answer, Janice steps into the living room. Deacon Julius smiles and shakes his head as he walks toward Janice and hands her the roses.

"Janice, you look beautiful."

"Thank you, you're looking sharp this evening. Kema, can

you put these in vase for me?"

"Yes, ma'am. I hope you all have a good time tonight."

Deacon Julius and Janice reply in unison without taking their eyes off each other, "We will." They walk arm-in-arm out of the door.

Kema removes the leaves from the stems and places the roses on the kitchen countertop. She looks through the cabinets to find a vase. Kema doesn't remember Janice ever having fresh flowers in the house while growing up. However, Granny Pauline used to place fresh flowers in a vase twice a year in remembrance of Grandpa William. Kema finds a vase in the back of a cabinet located above the stove's ventilation fan. Kema washes and rinses it with a mixture of baking soda and vinegar to reduce the bacteria in the vase and keep the roses from wilting quickly. Kema pours water into the vase, puts the roses in, and places the vase on the kitchen table.

Kema steps away from the table and admires the roses. Kema thinks, *Mama is going to feel so good seeing these on the table once she returns from her date*. Kema is tempted to stay until Janice returns to get all the details about her date. However, she doesn't want Janice to feel awkward if Deacon Julius wants to come inside when he brings her home. Kema chuckles at the thought of Mama inviting him in the house after the date. Romance is definitely in the air tonight.

*

As Kema is driving home, her cellphone rings. She looks at her dashboard display and sees that Sharon is calling her.

"Hey Sharon, Happy Valentine's Day!"

"Hey Kema. It sounds like you're driving. Are you on your way to meet a date?"

"No, I'm driving back home from Mama's house. I was helping *her* get ready for a date tonight."

"What? Ms. Janice has a date and we don't. Either the world must be coming to an end or we'll have better luck dating when we are in our sixties."

"I choose to believe we'll have better luck in the future."

"I was calling to see what you were doing tonight, but it sounds like your night is just as boring as mine. If you are up for company, I can bring some wine, pizza and cupcakes to eat while we watch a movie."

"We might as well eat, drink and be merry."

"Cool. I'll see you in about an hour and a half."

Sharon arrives with a bottle of sweet red wine, a large supreme thin crust pizza and red velvet cupcakes. Kema and Sharon eat the pizza and debate about whether to watch *Waiting to Exhale* or *Girls Trip*. They decide to watch *Girls Trip* because *Waiting to Exhale* reminds them too much of their single status, whereas *Girls Trip* is more upbeat and humorous.

Although Kema and Sharon have seen *Girls Trip* at least twice, they laugh like it's their first time watching it. Sharon's cellphone rings as the closing credits of the movie appear on the television screen.

Sharon looks at her phone and says, "Who could be calling me at this hour? Girl, it's Tony!"

"You still have his number."

"I keep it in my phone just in case."

"Just in case of what?

"Just in case of emergencies."

Kema looks at Sharon in disbelief, shakes her head and says: "I'm not even going to ask what type of emergencies Tony can handle."

Sharon places her phone in her purse, stumbles to stand up from the chair, and says, "Well, I guess I'm going to leave so you can get your rest."

"Are you sure you're okay driving? Let me get you a bottle of water."

"Yes, please and thank you."

Kema goes to the kitchen and retrieves a bottled water from the refrigerator. When she returns to the living room, she sees Sharon digging in her purse. Kema hands Sharon the water.

"Thank you, girl. Do you have an extra toothbrush?"

"Sure ... I guess this emergency meeting with Tony will involve some mouth-to-mouth resuscitation."

Sharon laughs and says, "Girl, you're crazy. I just want to make sure my breath isn't offensive."

"Look in the guest bathroom drawer closest to the sink and you'll find a travel-kit toothbrush and toothpaste."

Sharon grabs her purse and scurries to the guest bathroom. When she emerges fifteen minutes later, she has on a full face of makeup. Kema takes one look at her and says: "Girl, I thought that you fell in the toilet. If you'd stayed in there one minute more, I was going to knock on the door to check on you."

Kema locks the door after Sharon leaves, looks around her living room, and suddenly feels alone. She didn't expect Sharon to spend the entire night with her, but she certainly didn't expect her to leave for a date. Kema thinks, *would a booty call from an ex-boyfriend be considered a date? Kema, quit being jealous of your best friend.* Kema redirects her negative energy into cleaning up by removing the pizza box, cupcake container and wine bottle and glasses from the living room. After Kema cleans her place, her mind feels settled for a good night's rest.

CHAPTER 23

March 20, 2020

Mayor Tanya Braveheart joined Governor L.J. Alinsky to announce a state-wide order for Illinois residents to stay at home. The order requires all residents to remain at home unless traveling for essential needs and requires businesses not engaged in essential activities to only perform minimum operations. This order will occur on Saturday, March 21 at 5 p.m. and remain in place until the governor's disaster proclamation expires on April 7, 2020.

Kema's eyes widen and she covers her mouth with her hand as she sits in her office reading this advisory on her cellphone. Kema thinks, *just yesterday the news said Chicago only had a few COVID-19 cases. I should have known once the public schools closed that the situation was getting worse. We just had a profitable holiday season and now I have to close the store before five tomorrow. How will I make payroll?*

Kema stands up from behind the desk and walks to the storefront where Darron is standing behind the register looking at his cellphone.

"Darron, we have to close the store early tomorrow."

"Is it because of COVID-19? This should only last a week or two and we can open the store again."

"I hope that you are right."

"I don't think you should worry, Ms. Kema. Maybe it'll be a good break for us."

"It's slow in the store today. I guess people are shopping for food since Mayor Braveheart made her announcement. During these next two weeks, we really need to focus on improving the store's online presence."

"I can help with that. We can increase our Instagram ads, which will drive customers to our website."

"That's a good start Darron. I will call Antonio and give him an update."

Kema goes back to the office. Antonio answers the phone after the first ring; it's like he was anticipating her call.

They go through the pleasantries and then Kema says, "I'm calling to let you know that the store will be closed for at least two weeks due to the COVID-19 stay-at-home order. I plan to keep you and Darron on payroll during this time. Darron will be working on increasing our online presence through Instagram ads."

"I've been studying responsive web design on the side. I can improve the layout of Sweet Daddy's Fashions' website on smartphones and tablets."

"Antonio, that's a great idea. I will schedule a video conference for us next week to discuss our plans."

*

Kema, Darron and Antonio have the video conference on Monday and decide to run a two-week Instagram ad campaign. Nightclub and casualwear have been best sellers, however, since nightclubs and other social events are shuttered, the ads promote loungewear instead. Antonio explains how he will redesign the website using graphics and animation to highlight the sale and clearance items.

The two-week ad campaign is a success. Kema reviews the analytics and observes a fifty percent increase in traffic to the website and a thirty percent increase in online sales as compared to the previous weeks. The sale and clearance items sell out within the first week and loungewear is the best-selling category on the website.

Kema smiles, leans in closer to her laptop screen, and sets her peppermint tea on the kitchen table to review the analytics again. No, her mind isn't playing tricks on her. She will be able to make payroll this week without raiding her savings account.

Kema thinks, *not going into the store is not so bad after all. Once Mayor Braveheart announces that businesses can open up again during the press conference this afternoon, we will be alright.*

Kema has been so preoccupied with keeping the store afloat that she hasn't checked on Janice as frequently as she did before the COVID-19 stay-at-home order. Janice has only called her a handful of times since then. She figures Deacon Julius has been taking up Janice's time. Kema thinks, *maybe Deacon Julius is Mama's quarantine buddy?* Kema shakes her head and chuckles to herself at the preposterous thought. It took over twenty-five years for Janice to date someone, and it will likely take a few years before she even thinks about living with a man. Kema decides to call Janice to satisfy her curiosity.

"I just called to check in with you. I haven't seen you in over two weeks and wanted to stop by today. Do you need me to bring you anything?"

"Thank you, baby. I don't think it's a good idea to come over here since we are still on a stay-at home order."

"I understand that Mama. I won't stay long and I can wear a mask inside the house."

"I guess that will be fine."

"Okay, I will see you soon."

Kema is stunned by Janice's curt tone over the phone but thinks that once she sees Janice her demeanor will change. Kema looks at herself in the bathroom mirror as she folds a blue paisley print bandana into a mask and places it around her nose and mouth. With her hair pulled back into a bun, a jersey jogging suit, and no makeup or earrings, she thinks she looks as if she is preparing to rob a bank like the main characters in the movie *Set It Off*.

She puts on her black puffer coat, knit hat and insulated gloves and leaves the condo. Like Christmas Day, there's no traffic on the roads, so the twenty-minute commute to Janice's home only takes Kema fifteen minutes. Kema parks in front of Janice's house and walks to the door. Normally, she would use her key but with Janice's ambivalence about her arrival, she decides to knock.

Kema gives five playful knocks on the door. At least a minute passes before Janice opens the door without a mask on.

"Hi Mama!" Kema greets Janice as she walks in the house and attempts to hug her. Janice places her arm in front of her body as if she is a school crossing guard, blocking Kema.

"Hi Kema. The health officials say that we shouldn't be hugging anyone who does not live in our household."

"Okay, but I'm your daughter and I haven't been around anyone since the lockdown."

"I'd rather be safe than sorry. They say that I am at high risk because of my age."

Janice walks to the couch and sits down. Kema attempts to sit down on the opposite end of the couch. Janice shakes her head "no" and points to the gray rocking chair on the other side of the living room.

Kema takes of her coat, sits in the chair and rocks back and forth looking around the room and then at Janice before she asks, "How have you been?"

"I've been doing alright. Trying to keep up with what's going on with the virus. How are you making it with the store being closed?"

"I've been able to make payroll because of the team's diligence. We moved all the stores sales online and placed advertisements on social media. Once the store opens up next week, I have a good feeling we'll do well."

"I doubt that we'll be back to normal anytime soon. I received an automated voice call from the church. Do you remember Sister Lillian?"

Kema places her hand to her head as she thinks and replies, "Yes, the lady who keeps up with my church attendance."

"Don't be ugly Kema. The call from the church said that she passed away from COVID-19."

Kema immediately feels shameful over her comment and says, "I'm sorry, Mama."

"I just talked to her last week and she was thinking that

she had a cold. She was letting her grandson stay with her after his mother kicked him out of the house for smoking weed. I don't know why she would allow him to live with her. If he was grown enough to smoke weed, he could live on his own. He probably gave her COVID as he was always ripping and running in the streets."

Kema jumps up from the rocking chair, startled, as a deep voice coming from the hall asks, "Janice, who's ripping and running in the streets?"

Janice looks embarrassed as Deacon Julius, wearing a tight-fitting white t-shirt, red jogging pants and slippers, emerges from the hall into the living room.

"Hello Deacon Julius. Mama didn't tell me you were here."

Janice grits her teeth, turns to Deacon Julius before he can reply to Kema and says, "Julius, I told you to stay in my room."

"I felt claustrophobic in there by myself, jaybird. And I needed a snack."

Kema thinks, *Jaybird? I hope he hasn't given her that nickname because she walks naked as a jaybird through the house.*

"Give me a few more minutes with Kema, dumpling."

Deacon Julius lowers his head and replies dejectedly as he shuffles towards the kitchen, "Alright … nice to see you Kema."

Kema and Janice sit in silence until Deacon Julius walks back to the bedroom.

"So … are you and Deacon Julius living together?"

"He's staying here until the stay-at-home-order is lifted. He didn't want me traveling back and forth to his place."

"I see … Is he the reason that you were hesitant about me coming over?"

"Kema, you've been so busy running the store that I barely hear from you. Julius suggested that I give you your space."

"Well, I won't hold you up from enjoying the rest of your day with Deacon Dumpling, I mean, Deacon Julius."

Kema expects Janice to chastise her for her comment, but Janice just laughs as she stands up from the couch and says, "It was good seeing you. We'll talk later."

Kema gets into the car and instead of turning on her music from her playlist on her phone she puts on the local news radio and hears the following announcement:

Governor L.J. Alinsky has extended the state-wide order for Illinois residents to stay at home. The order will keep residents off the streets and close most businesses until May 30, 2020.

Kema looks up at the roof of her car, then back down to the steering wheel and grips it tightly before starting the car to drive back home.

CHAPTER 24

May 4, 2020

"Girl, I don't know why it took you so long to apply for the PPP loan. You have employees who have bills to pay just like you. There is no shame in applying for a loan. I took out a $20,000 loan to start my first beauty shop. I wasn't in debt for long because I had a plan to pay the loan off in six months. Call me back, please."

Kema is in bed listening to the voicemail that Sharon left on her cellphone. Sharon received funds from the Paycheck Protection Program (PPP loan) in March for her beauty shops and encouraged Kema to apply for it too. Kema applied for it in mid-April and doesn't know the status of the loan. She needs another option.

After tossing and turning all night long, Kema drags her weary body out of the bed around nine and types on her laptop "Best place to sell a Porsche 911" in the online search engine. Her stomach is in knots. This is the first week since the pandemic began that she is nervous about paying her team. Kema hopes that she'll have at least six months payroll when she sells her car. Her savings are now allocated to paying her mortgage on the condo and other living expenses. Downsizing to another condo now is not feasible because Chicago is sheltering in place. Placing her belongings in storage and moving in with Janice is not possible either because she needs her privacy and doesn't want to hear unsolicited advice or Janice saying, "I told you not to give up your good job". Also, there's Janice's houseguest and Kema isn't interested in staying there long enough to know the origin of their pet names for each other.

Kema clicks on a website link "wetakeyourluxcar.com". To get a valuation, she places her car's mileage, year, make, model and condition in the online form. To her surprise, her car is valued at $81,500. Kema thinks, *for this amount of money, I can learn to ride the bus again.* Kema calls the salesperson listed on the website to find out more information.

"Hello, Steven Kaatz speaking."

"Hello, Steven. My name is Kema Daniels. I just received an online valuation for my Porsche 911 and I'd like to set up an appointment to inspect my car.

"Great! Just one second. Let me look up your information in our database. How is your morning going so far?"

Kema is annoyed that he's not solely focused on finding her information, but manages to push her feelings to the side and replies, "My morning is going well, thank you."

"Good, good, good. Found it! You're in luck because this car is in high demand. For your convenience, I can perform the inspection at your home and if it goes well, I will present you with a check for your vehicle afterwards. I'll wear my mask during the inspection and stand six feet away from you while speaking. My next available appointment is this Wednesday at 11:00 a.m."

"Wednesday at eleven is fine."

"Perfect. If you need to cancel or reschedule the appointment please call or text me."

Kema feels like she has just swallowed a boulder. She is two days away from giving up her dream car. Kema thinks, *this can't be life.* Kema has a video conference scheduled with her team at 10:00 a.m. to discuss the marketing goals for the upcoming week. However, thirty minutes before the meeting she gets back in bed and sends a group text to her team cancelling it and reschedules it for 10:00 on Tuesday.

Exercise is usually Kema's remedy for when she is feeling sad, but she can't muster the energy for one leg lift. She tells herself that she needs just one more hour in bed to rest and then she will start her day. The one hour of rest turns into three hours.

Kema's eyes spring open as a text alert on her cellphone awakens her at 1:00 p.m. The text alert is for a local news article with the title "Out of PPEs: Gorreta Hospital Staff Scramble for Solutions". Kema glances at the headline but doesn't enter her password into her phone to read the article. She stretches her arms up to the ceiling and extends her legs out of the bed as she slowly gets out of the bed. Kema has no appetite and walks past the kitchen to her dining room table where her laptop is located. She logs into the store's email and clicks on an email entitled "PPP Loan Decision Notice".

Ms. Kema Daniels (Sweet Daddy's Fashions):

This notice is provided both to the entity identified above ("Applicant"), which applied for a Paycheck Protection Program Loan from Umbra Bank, and the individual identified above ("Authorized Representative"). The details of the application are provided below.

After careful consideration of your application, we regret that we cannot extend credit to the Applicant at this time for the following reason(s):

    1.   Funds are not available.

If you have any questions regarding this notice, visit https://support.umbrabank.com

Sincerely,
Umbra Bank

      Kema lowers her head and thinks: *instead of being skeptical about the PPP loan, I should have applied at the same time as Sharon. Well, there was no guarantee that I would have received the loan if I had applied for it early. At least I can cross out the PPP loan as an option.*

*

It's Tuesday morning. Kema chokes down a half-ripe banana and follows it with a cup of peppermint tea before she meets with her team by video conference. She brushes her hair into a bun, slaps on nude color lipstick, and puts on a dark gray blazer over an off-white camisole, paired with navy-blue sweatpants. Taking the extra effort to put on dress pants is exhausting for Kema. She counts it a victory that she has enough energy to make the upper half of her body presentable. Darron and Antonio are already on the video conference when Kema logs in.

After they greet, Kema begins, "I apologize for canceling yesterday on short notice and appreciate your willingness to meet this morning. I'm going to keep the call brief so we all can get back to work. It seems that this pandemic will not end as soon as we would like. I want to keep you aware of what I have been doing to ensure that we receive a paycheck this week. I applied for a PPP loan but was denied because the loan program no longer has funds. I have another plan that will allow us to run our business for up to six months."

"What's the plan?" Darron asks.

"I can't disclose it yet. Don't worry it is nothing illegal," Kema says while laughing.

Darron and Antonio give a nervous chuckle and all three are silent for about five seconds before Kema continues.

"Darron, post to Instagram once a day instead of every other day. The material that you post can be inspirational and motivational posts to let our customers know that we are here for them and working hard behind the scenes ... Better yet ... let's take a screen shot of our meeting and post it."

"Yeah, Ms. Kema, we can let our customers know that we haven't stopped grinding," Darron replies.

"Antonio, this week I want you to make sure that all the weblinks are functional on our website."

"I can do that," Antonio replies.

"Gentlemen, do you have any questions or concerns?"

"No, I know what we need to do," Darron says.

"Thank you! Contact me by text or phone if you have any questions."

Kema ends the video conference and goes to her bedroom to change into a hooded sweatshirt that matches her sweatpants. She leaves her condo to get her car washed and interior vacuumed before the car inspection the next day. Kema enters the car and before she starts it up, she places her head down on the steering wheel and tears start streaming. This will be the last ride in her dream car.

CHAPTER 25

"We no longer need your vehicle model. I'm sorry that I didn't get to tell you earlier. Since we last spoke, our company has received a surplus of Porsche 911s. It looks like the pandemic has prompted many to cut back on their expenses. I'll let you know in two months if we need your vehicle," Steven Kaatz says.

"Two months? I need to have this car sold today. Can you recommend any other luxury car brokers?"

"Sorry, our company's policy doesn't permit us to recommend competitors."

"That's funny … But it is your company's policy to wait until the last minute to tell customers that the company can't provide a service?"

"Again, I'm sorry for the inconvenience."

Kema's face burns as if she were outside in sweltering heat. She cuts the call and starts pacing the floor in the living room. After about five minutes, she sits down on the sofa and turns on the television. The local morning news is on and the anchor person is interviewing healthcare staff from Gorreta Hospital. Kema is about to change the channel until she sees a familiar face on the screen. Nurse Angela, the nurse who informed Kema and Linda about the passing of Benjamin, Kema's father, appears on the screen and says:

"Because of the manufacturing shortage of personal protective equipment, we are reusing our disposable gowns and face masks if we think we have not come in contact with COVID-19 patients. This is not safe for our patients, staff or our families. I'm living in the basement of my home because I'm afraid that I will expose my fam-

*ily to the virus. If you have purchased extra face masks or can make
them, please consider donating them to healthcare facilities."*

Suddenly, Kema has an idea. Chicago is only allowing essential businesses to open their store fronts. If Sweet Daddy's Fashions sells gowns and face masks, it would be considered an essential business. Kema thinks, *how can I acquire gowns and face masks? Linda is a seamstress! Maybe she can make the gowns and masks.* Kema calls Linda.

"Hello, Kema. How are you?"

"Hi, Linda. I'd like to say that I'm doing good, but I wouldn't be telling you the truth."

"What's going on?"

"To make a long story short, I don't know how I'm going to make payroll for my team. I need your help on an idea that I have that will make a significant impact on the healthcare workers ..."

"I know that this pandemic has been difficult for business. Have you applied for a PPP loan?"

"Yes, I have but no luck. I also tried to sell my car to cover payroll but the company that I was going to sell it to told me that they no longer wanted it."

"I'm so sorry Kema. How can I help you with your idea?"

"Gorreta Hospital has run out of disposable masks and gowns and are requesting donations. Would you be interested in making masks and gowns to help?"

"Kema, I've never made masks or gowns before. I don't think I would be able to do it."

"There must be instructions online? They have tutorials for just about everything now."

"At my age, I don't think I'm up to it. I'm enjoying my retirement and the extra downtime that I have due to the shelter-in-place order."

"Do you remember Nurse Angela? She was the nurse who was with us when Daddy passed away. She was on television this morning saying that the healthcare workers are risking their health and safety by reusing disposable masks and gowns.

I think Gorreta Hospital staff really looked out for Daddy during his hospital stays and I think we should do what we can to support them."

Linda pauses before saying, "Okay you've convinced me. I'll also ask my sister, nieces and nephews to assist."

*

Kema calls Gorreta Hospital and is directed to Ashley Givens, the community relations manager. Ashley is enthusiastic about Kema offering to donate the personal protective equipment. She asks Kema for her email address to send her a website link containing instructions on how to make medical face masks and isolation gowns.

Kema clicks on the link and watches the instructional video and thinks, *I'm sure Linda can sew the masks and gowns, and if I watch the video a few more times, I can probably do it too!*

Kema spends the rest of the day contacting Sweet Daddy's Fashions clothing manufacturers to see if they are interested in donating fabric for the cause. Four out of the ten manufacturers contacted can provide the donation. The other manufacturers are already using their fabric to produce personal protective equipment for other hospitals in the United States.

After a productive day, Kema decides to go to get ready for bed at nine. She hears her cellphone ring as she walks to her room. It's Sharon.

"Hello?"

"Kema, are you screening your calls? You didn't call me back. What's going on?"

"I'm sorry. I have been in a funk trying to figure out how to keep the store afloat."

"You didn't get the PPP loan?"

"No. Then I tried to sell my car through a luxury car brokerage company but couldn't because all of a sudden the company didn't need my car model anymore."

"Selling your car? There's a reason it didn't work out. Kema, you don't sacrifice your personal property to keep a business."

"I don't know what else to do ..."

"You should have asked me instead of trying to be "Ms. Independent". Have you used your business line of credit or applied for a business term loan?"

"No. I'm trying to avoid getting into any debt."

"Kema, knowing your personality, you will pay off any debt before the interest accumulates ... On another note, I need your business to be open so Cassandra can have something to do for a few hours. She is driving my sister crazy."

"Cassandra? Isn't she still at the University of Wisconsin?"

"No, she decided to quarantine at home and take classes online. After this semester, she will transfer to the University of Illinois-Chicago. No need to pay out-of-state fees when she can't have the traditional on-campus experience."

"Can Cassandra sew?"

"No. But, she should learn what it takes to make the designer clothes she loves to wear. What do you have in mind?"

"Sweet Daddy's Fashions will manufacture and donate face masks and gowns to Gorreta Hospital. Because Linda is a seamstress, I asked her to help me and I received an instructional video from the hospital on how to make them."

"Girl, count Cassandra in. Even if all she can do is sort the fabric and cut it."

"Thank you, Sharon. I missed talking to you and I promise to be a better friend by staying in contact."

"I'll let it slide this time because I know how stressful running a business can be. Fortunately, I'm able to pay my staff with the PPP loan, but I have to admit that I will be concerned if this stay-at-home order lasts throughout the summer. There will be a whole lot of angry, frizzy-haired women."

"Ha-ha! You're describing the way that I look now. I've had my laugh for the night and can go to sleep with a smile. Good night, Sharon."

Kema hangs up the phone and instead of going to sleep,

she searches online how to social distance in two thousand
square feet of retail space.

CHAPTER 26

"Thank you all for your willingness to support our healthcare workers at Gorreta Hospital. I believe our efforts here will have a strong positive impact on our community that we will look back and be proud of for many years to come."

The storefront erupts in applause and muffled cheers through masks as Kema finishes addressing her volunteer team consisting of Darron, Antonio, Cassandra, Linda, Linda's sister Camila, Linda's niece Jasmine and nephew Pedro.

The storefront's interior has been transformed. The clothing racks and mannequins have been placed along the walls. Four folding tables that serve as work areas for assembling the face masks and gowns, are in the center of the floor. Darron and Cassandra are sorting the pallets filled with fabrics at the first table. Antonio and Kema are cutting the fabrics to the specified lengths at the second table, Camila and Jasmine are stationed at the third table, which contains two sewing machines. Camila sews the gowns and Jasmine sews the face masks. Linda serves as quality control by inspecting the gowns and masks and Pedro irons the gowns and face masks and places them in separate containers to be delivered to the hospital.

The first day is stressful for the team. Linda sends back three gowns and ten face masks for reassembly because either the gowns were a half inch longer than the specification or the pleats in the face mask were not evenly spaced. Kema humbly accepts the constructive criticism, but Camila and Linda get into a family quarrel and speak in Spanish to each other. To prevent more errors, Linda decides to watch each table and correct the team members before the gowns and face masks arrive at her table for the final inspection. The second and third days go by much more smoothly as the team becomes more comfortable in their roles. After four days, the team has assembled one hundred gowns and one hundred face masks that are ready to be delivered to the hospital.

Because Kema's car isn't spacious enough to transport the face masks and gowns, Pedro loads them in his large SUV with Kema riding beside him in the front seat. Pedro turns on the radio and the music fills the silence between them. Once they arrive at the loading area entrance of the hospital, Kema calls Ashley Givens to let her know they've arrived. Ashley walks to the SUV to greet them.

"Hello, you must be Kema! It's so nice to meet you in person."

"Hello, Ashley. It's nice to meet you too." Kema turns toward Pedro and says: "Ashley, this is Pedro. He has graciously volunteered his time and SUV to deliver the gowns and face masks."

"Nice to meet you Pedro and thank you for your generosity." Ashley anxiously looks at Pedro and Kema before saying: "I wish I could shake both of your hands but this pandemic is preventing any type of social contact."

"Pleasure to meet you, Ashley. I prefer vocal greetings over handshakes anyway," Pedro replies.

Kema is surprised by Pedro's response considering he has been as quiet as the sound of an earring falling from a lady's ear. Ashley uses her walkie talkie to request assistance at the loading dock. In less than a minute, two tall, masked men arrive and remove the boxes of gowns and face masks from the SUV. Kema and Pedro get back in the SUV and wave goodbye to Ashley. During the ride back to the store, Kema attempts to strike up a conversation with Pedro.

"Thank you again, Pedro for all of your help this week. Are you in school or do you work?"

"I used to work as a hotel concierge at The Promontory.

This year was my year to get a raise but I was laid off in March and haven't been able to find another job. Tía Linda, I'm sorry, Aunt Linda, said that while I am looking for a job, I need to do something to keep my mind occupied.

"I'm sorry to hear about your job. This pandemic has changed all of our lifestyles. I would have still been hiding my head under my bed sheets worried about the store closing if Linda had not agreed to assist and ask you and your family members to join me. I don't know what will come out of this but I feel good knowing that we have helped others in their time of need."

"Good karma will soon come."

"Yes, I hope it will come soon."

*

It's Friday. Two days have passed since she and Pedro delivered the face masks and gowns to Gorreta Hospital. Helping Gorreta Hospital was a good distraction from the reality that Kema has to make payroll next Friday and she hasn't yet figured it out. She decides to obtain a business loan through an online company.

"A thirty percent interest rate and $250 pre-payment penalty for a two-year business loan is absurd. We have been in business for over twenty years … The business credit score is forty-five? This must be a mistake."

"This is what our records show Ms. Daniels. During this time, this is the best online loan that we can offer. You can agree to the terms to process the loan by digitally signing the form. If you decide you don't want the loan, you can cancel before forty-eight hours without a penalty."

Kema tugs her earlobes in disbelief. She exhales deeply before replying, "When will the money arrive in the business account?"

"It should arrive in two business days."

"I will sign the form this afternoon."

"Thank you. Call or send an email if you have any other questions."

Kema ends the call without saying goodbye. She's in shock and feels as if the walls are closing in on her. Kema needs to talk to someone. Calling Janice is not an option because she wouldn't understand what she's going through. Sharon's probably busy and wouldn't be able to talk right away. She digitally signs the loan contract and places the attachment in an email. Kema's cellphone rings and she looks at the screen, noticing it's Gorreta Hospital.

"Hello? This is Kema Daniels."

"Hello, Ms. Daniels. This is Dr. Richard Murphy, CEO of Gorreta Hospital. How are you?"

"I'm doing well thank you."

"I'm calling to personally thank you and your team for manufacturing the face masks and gowns for our staff. You have helped solve an enormous issue the hospital has been plagued with. Would you be interested in a six-month contract with us to manufacture more face masks and gowns?"

"Yes, I'd be interested," Kema says without any hesitation.

"That's fantastic! Priscilla Thompson, our chief financial officer, will call you at 2:00 p.m. today to discuss the details of the contract. Thank you again for your assistance."

"Thank you, Dr. Murphy."

Kema looks up at the ceiling, points her right index finger, and shouts: "Thank you Lord! You are so faithful."

She deletes the draft email that contained the attachment of the signed loan contract and walks into the kitchen to get a glass of water. Her appetite has diminished because of her worries about the store. Kema thinks that once she speaks with Priscilla Thompson, her appetite will return.

Priscilla calls as promised. Kema tells her that she has a seven-member team involved in the manufacturing of the gowns and face masks. Mrs. Thompson says that the hospital is expecting five thousand face masks and five thousand gowns to be delivered during the six months. The total compensation will be $50,000. The hospital will pay 50% within two business days of signing the contract and the remaining balance once all the face masks and gowns are delivered. Mrs. Thompson sends the contract to Kema by email and Kema reads, digitally signs, and emails the contract back to her.

Kema quickly realizes that the two consumer sewing machines that her team has been using will not be sufficient. Searching online, she finds three commercial second-hand sewing machines for $1500 each. Kema pays $200 extra for expedited delivery by Tuesday. She has a video conference with the team on Monday and discusses the contract and how they will be compensated for their work. Pedro, Antonio and Darron set up the sewing machines on Tuesday to allow the team to begin work on Wednesday.

On Wednesday morning, Kema wakes up before her 5:00 a.m. alarm, dresses herself, and leaves her home. She stops at the grocery store to pick up a fruit tray, bananas, bottled water and protein bars. Then, she stops at Doughman's Donuts to pick up donuts and coffee. When Kema arrives at the store at seven, she strategically arranges the breakfast items. From left to right, Kema places napkins, forks and plates on the table followed by donuts, bananas, fruit tray, protein bars and bottled water.

The team arrives at eight and devours the food in less time than it took her to arrange it. Before the team starts working, Linda inspects the sewing machines ensuring the belts are not worn and the bobbin winders are properly aligned. The machines pass Linda's inspection and she playfully chastises Kema for not consulting her before purchasing them. The team produces one thousand face masks and one thousand gowns the first week and Kema projects they will complete the order before six months. The second week Kema encourages the team members to cross-train in different areas each week just in case someone is unable to report to work. Kema notices that Cassandra has been willing to cross-train, however, she notices that she lingers around the fabric-cutting work area and has not joined Camila and Jasmine's sewing station on week three.

"Cassandra, may I speak with you by the front door?" Kema asks.

"Sure," Cassandra replies.

"I noticed that you haven't joined Camila and Jasmine to learn how to sew the face masks and gowns. Are you feeling okay today?"

"I feel fine. It's just … I don't think I'll be any good at sewing and I don't want Ms. Linda and her family to be angry with me if I mess up."

"Making mistakes is part of the learning process. Last week, I had to demonstrate to them that I could sew at least three face masks and three gowns before I was allowed to operate the sewing machines on my own."

"During our first week, I saw Ms. Linda and Ms. Camila arguing and I don't want to get cursed out. Especially in a language that I don't understand."

"No worries. You won't be scolded on my watch."

Cassandra nods at Kema and slowly walks over to Camila and Jasmine. While Kema is ironing the face masks, she observes Cassandra and Jasmine talking and laughing while Camila is changing a bent needle on the sewing machine. By the end of the day, Cassandra has sewn twenty face masks and runs up to Kema like a proud daughter showing off her art project.

"Ms. Kema, our team should have uniform masks that display Sweet Daddy's Fashions. I'm picturing a white background with black silhouettes of a man in a suit, a woman in a dress and a man in a hoodie."

"I think that's a good idea, but I don't think we'll have time to make face masks for the team."

"I talked to Ms. Linda and she said I can take home her personal sewing machine and make the masks after work."

"Well, since you have Ms. Linda's support, I agree to this project."

"Thank you!" Cassandra replies as she turns on her heels.

Three days later, Cassandra arrives at the store with the face masks. The team puts the masks on and Cassandra suggests that they take a picture. However, this picture is not your ordinary "snap a quick group selfie picture with your cellphone".

Cassandra asks Darron to retrieve a ladder from the storage area. Kema looks perplexed about why a ladder is needed to take a picture until she sees Cassandra climbing the six-foot ladder like a construction worker and leans the cell phone in the crevice of the top cap of the ladder. She sets the camera timer for three minutes. Cassandra gingerly steps from the ladder to ensure she does not knock over the phone. She lines the team up for the photo in the shape of an arrow. Kema is in the front row, Linda, Camila and Jasmine are in the second row, Cassandra and Darron are in the third row, and Pedro and Antonio are in the fourth row. Ten seconds after Cassandra positions herself to the left of Darron, the cell phone camera takes the photo.

Cassandra climbs the ladder again to get her phone. Once she is back on the floor, she looks at the picture and passes the phone around so everyone can see.

Darron looks at the picture and says, "We should post this on Instagram with the caption: *Sweet Daddy's Fashions committed to fighting COVID by supplying quality PPEs to healthcare workers.*"

"Excellent ideas! We've been so busy working that we have neglected our social media presence. We should post a photo or short video of our activities at least every other day to keep our customers engaged," Kema says.

Cassandra sends the photo to the teams group text chat and Darron posts the photo with the caption and hashtags to Instagram. Darron checks Instagram before the team stops working for the day and notices that the post has received over twenty thousand views and five hundred comments. Most of the comments are from people inquiring if the face masks are for sale.

Darron puts his right fist over his mask and says: "Oh wow! People on Instagram are asking where they can purchase the masks."

Cassandra scrambles to get her phone from her jeans pocket, looks at the post, and says, "It looks like I'll be busy after work."

"Correction, we'll be busy. You were the catalyst for this

initiative but we won't let you burn out fulfilling the demand for face masks. We are a team and we'll work together," Kema says.

Darron creates an Instagram post stating that a limited supply of face masks will be available for sale for $10 next Friday between three and five in the afternoon. The post requests that anyone who purchases the masks take a picture and post it to Instagram with the hashtag #SweetDaddysFashions.

The team works two hours overtime each day to produce 200 face masks. On Friday, around 2:30 p.m. there is a line of about thirty people waiting to purchase the face masks. The face masks are sold out by four. Darron collects the email and phone numbers of the disappointed customers on the store's tablet. He assures them that they will be notified first to purchase the masks once they are produced.

The next week the team works for twelve hours Monday to Friday and produces five hundred face masks. Kema tells the team that they will sell four hundred face masks and donate one hundred face masks to the homeless shelter, Faithful Haven. Darron emails the customers who were waiting for the face masks to be made and gives them a day head start to purchase the masks online and pick them up at the store. Then he makes another post on Instagram advertising that the masks will be sold again and one hundred face masks will be donated to Faithful Haven.

The store sells out of the masks again within an hour with some customers purchasing masks to donate to Faithful Haven. Since the team has worked diligently for the past two weeks and is caught up with the face masks and gowns for Gorreta Hospital, Kema gives the team Saturday off. As Kema exits the store to walk to her car, she sees a man and a woman wearing Sweet Daddy's Fashions face masks. They nod their heads to greet Kema as they pass by. She continues walking to her car feeling light as a feather, yet heavy with joy and gratitude for what her team has accomplished. Her cell phone rings as she opens the car door. Before she starts the car, she removes her cell phone from her purse and sees a missed call and voicemail from

Wendy Sullivan.

Kema thinks, *it's been over six months since I left Resilient Financial. Why would Wendy be calling me now?*

CHAPTER 27

Once Kema arrives home, her curiosity gets the best of her. Instead of eating her dinner first, she decides to return Wendy's call. Kema thinks it's better to hear what Wendy has to say on an empty stomach. Wendy answers after the third ring. Once they have greeted each other and discussed the pandemic, Wendy starts to explain the reason for her call.

"Kema, you're much too modest. I heard that you're the owner of Sweet Pop's Fashions. How's business going?"

"The name of the store is Sweet Daddy's Fashions and it's doing great."

"I was concerned considering that Mayor Braveheart and the governor have closed all non-essential businesses that your little store is a bit stuck. Did you get a PPP loan?"

"Again, business is fine. I just returned home from the store and I'm exhausted. Is there anything I can help you with Wendy?"

"I was just checking on you and I wanted to say how proud I am of you for taking a chance and becoming an entrepreneur. I wish I was as courageous as you are but I'm addicted to a steady paycheck. Truth be told I don't know how steady my paycheck will be in the next few weeks. Resilient Financial has laid off half of the research analysts and associates and let Lauren McCullough go. Can you believe it? She was doing so well in your old position. I questioned Mr. Reynolds about the decision to lay off Lauren and he simply told me that the board made the decision to protect the company's profitability."

"I'm sorry to hear that. I'm sure Lauren will land on her

feet soon. I really must be…"

"Wait, before you hang up, I want to apologize to you. I'm sorry for not being a good mentor to you. Heck, I probably should call Lauren and apologize to her as well."

"Yes, you probably should. Take care Wendy."

Kema smirks to herself and goes to the kitchen and prepares spaghetti, salad and garlic bread. She enjoys the comforting meal on the couch as she watches television. Kema has not relaxed in weeks and quickly falls asleep thirty minutes into watching *Law & Order: SVU*.

Kema spends the weekend resting without checking her business email and has renewed energy for Monday morning. Soon after Kema sits down at her desk, she sees an email from Olivia Crenshaw, the CEO of Stellar Apparel. She is hesitant to click on it because it could be a phishing email but she takes a couple of calming breaths, she clicks on the email.

Dear Ms. Daniels

My team and I have been following Sweet Daddy's Fashions posts on Instagram and are pleased to see that your organization provides personal protective equipment to healthcare workers and donates masks to the less fortunate. This has encouraged us to follow your lead here in New York City. Although the pandemic has affected business as usual, we are fortunate enough to still be expanding our business domestically. We would like to speak with you about partnering with us. Please reply to this email at your earliest convenience.

I hope to hear from you soon.

Sincerely,

Olivia Crenshaw
CEO Stellar Apparel

Kema can't believe what she's reading so has to re-read the email three times to convince herself it's real. Then she sends a reply stating she would be interested in learning more about a partnership with Stellar Apparel. She thinks the worst that could happen is that she won't get a response. But if she does and the email is asking for money or personal information, she'll simply block the sender.

Kema decides not to tell anyone about the email until she knows more. She checks her inbox at lunch time and sees that Olivia has responded to her requesting a video conference on Wednesday. Kema thinks, *oh my goodness. This is for real.*

Linda is the only person that Kema can trust to give her sound advice. When Linda returns from her lunch break, Kema asks her to come to the office to discuss business.

"Linda, I think Stellar Apparel wants to acquire Sweet Daddy's Fashions!"

"Qué?"

"Olivia Crenshaw, the CEO of Stellar Apparel, sent an email to me about a partnership with her company and re- quested a video conference with me on Wednesday at noon with her team. You're the first person I've told. Please keep this be- tween us."

"Kema, this is exciting news, but are you sure the email was from her? Also, are you sure you want to sell the business? Usually when an acquisition occurs the acquired company loses its staff."

"If I decide to sell, I'll make sure that doesn't happen. Most of my career at Resilient Financial was spent evaluating and leading a team in company mergers and acquisitions. I will per- form due diligence before making any decision."

*

"Pedro, I'm sorry that you don't feel well today. Please get tested. You can return to work once you show me paperwork of your negative results."

Kema ends the call and paces back and forth praying for a solution to her dilemma.

It's Wednesday morning and Pedro is scheduled to deliver the gowns and face masks to Gorreta Hospital. Today is also the day that Kema meets with Stellar Apparel via video conference.

Who is she going to find with a truck to make the delivery on such short notice?

Kema thinks, *delivery ... delivery ... Joseph! I don't have his number but I think I remember the name of the company that he works for.* Kema looks at the last delivery invoice and sees the name of the company and a phone number. Kema dials without hesitation.

"J Transporters, this is Joseph speaking."

"Hello, Joseph. This is Kema Daniels from Sweet Daddy's Fashions. It's so good to hear your voice. How are you?"

"Hello, Ms. Kema. I'm doing alright. Business has been slow from this pandemic but we're hanging in there."

"I'm sorry to call you last minute but one of my team members is ill and I need to have gowns and face masks delivered to Gorreta Hospital at 11:00 this morning. Are you able to do it?"

"Sure, P.B. and I can come by the store at ten for pick up."

"What's the cost?"

"How many boxes do you have?"

"Six."

"How much does each box weigh?"

"Approximately ten pounds per box."

"$200 for delivery plus $15 a box ... The total is $290."

"Thank you, you're a life saver Joseph."

Kema is anxious for Joseph and P.B. to arrive and decides to wait outside. They get to the store ten minutes before ten. Joseph gets out of the truck first and P.B. follows right behind him and waves at Kema. Kema can only imagine his silly grin through his white mask. As Joseph takes confident strides towards Kema, she notices his brown deep-set eyes and biceps bursting through his red polo shirt. She wants to look away but she can't. The pandemic has been kind to his physique.

Joseph wipes his brow with his forearm and says, "Good morning, Ms. Kema. It's too hot and humid for you to be standing out here."

P.B. rocks back and forth from one foot to the next seconding Joseph's observation by saying, "Yeah, Ms. Kema. What are you doing out here?"

"Good morning, gentlemen. Yes, it is hot out here. Let's go inside and I'll show you the boxes that need to be delivered."

Joseph and P.B. follow Kema inside the store and observe how the store has transformed into a miniature manufacturing facility.

"Wow … the pandemic has got y'all making clothes now," P.B. says.

"Man, do you ever think before you speak?" Joseph says.

Kema laughs and replies, "No, P.B. we've been making masks and gowns for the healthcare workers at Gorreta Hospital. I'm grateful you can deliver the supplies to the hospital today."

With a gleam in his eye, Joseph says, "It's our pleasure Ms. Kema. You can call us anytime you need our assistance."

"I appreciate that," Kema replies and feels relieved that Joseph can't see her blushing through her mask.

"Where can I get one of those Sweet Daddy's Fashions masks?" P.B. says abruptly.

"We've sold out but, if we decide to make more, I'll let you know," Kema replies.

Joseph and P.B. load the six boxes in the truck and as soon as Joseph closes the hatch in the back of the truck, Kema hands Joseph $300 in cash.

"I don't have any change at the moment, but I can …"

"Keep the change. You're doing me a huge favor."

"Thank you!" Joseph says as he tucks the money in his pants pocket.

Kema watches him walk to the driver's side and pictures him without his shirt on. Her lustful daydream is disrupted when P.B. sticks his head out of the passenger side window and shouts:

"Bye, Ms. Kema!"

CHAPTER 28

"$800,000 is Stellar Apparel's offer for Sweet Daddy's Fashions," Kema says in disgust.

Linda pauses on the phone for what seems like an eternity before responding, "Well, Kema. What price were you expecting? Did they propose keeping all of the employees?"

"At least 1.5 million. Yes, they agreed to keep our employees because they are acquiring us only to expand their financial portfolio. However, only Darron and Antonio are full-time employees. I don't want to leave out Jasmine, Pedro, Camila and Cassandra who are working as independent contractors right now because of the contract with Gorreta Hospital."

"I'm certain Camila doesn't want to become an employee of Sweet Daddy's Fashions. She enjoys retirement and is only working on this contract to support the healthcare workers. I can't speak for the others."

"I've been given a week to either accept or counter the offer. I thought I could negotiate by myself but I need a lawyer."

"Did you contact the lawyer who helped us with the purchasing agreement paperwork?"

"Bradley Davis? Yes. I called him but he hasn't returned any of my calls."

"Have you called Victor to see if he can help?"

Kema's stomach sinks. It's been several months and she is still not over Victor. Kema swallows hard and replies, "No, I'm not sure if I still have his number." Kema thinks, *Lord forgive me for telling this lie.*

"Hold on a second. I have his cell number saved in my

phone."

Kema shuffles some papers around as if she is looking for a pen and says, "I'm ready".

Kema ends the call with Linda and instead of calling Victor, she scrolls through her news feed on her phone. After about ten minutes of reading, she goes to her contact list and finds Victor's number.

Kema gives herself a quick pep talk. *Alright Kema, quit procrastinating and call him.*

She selects his number and presses the call button. Victor answers after the third ring.

"Hello. This is Victor Pennington."

Kema doesn't reply. Her mouth is as dry as the desert. She coughs to force words to come out of her mouth.

"Hello?" Victor replies.

"Hi Victor. This is Kema. How have you been?"

"Kema ..."

Kema thinks, *I know this man is not pretending like he doesn't know who I am. He's being really petty. I should just hang up now.* However, Kema needs his assistance and decides to reply and not let her feelings take over.

"Kema Daniels"

"No! The same Kema Daniels who told me she no longer wanted to pursue a relationship with me?"

"Apparently, it didn't take you very long to move on. You were giggling with another woman and acting like I was an acquaintance that day Linda and I were signing the paperwork for the purchasing agreement."

"Kema, you didn't leave me any choice. I called you repeatedly to explain the situation to you but you were not trying to hear me."

"I'm sorry. I didn't call you to rehash old issues. I called because I need your professional help."

"I'll help you if you promise to finally listen to me."

Kema lets out a sigh and says, "Okay. I'm listening."

"The panties that you saw in my bathroom that night

were Griselle's."

"You *were* dating Griselle and me at the same time."

"No, I wasn't. She and I became friends when I first started taking salsa dance lessons. Griselle didn't have a car so I would drop her off at her place after my dance lesson. The night before we planned to go out, she called and told me that the water was cut off at her apartment and she really needed to take a shower and use my sink to wash some small items. I picked her up, let her use the guest bathroom and dropped her off the same night. I didn't check to see if she left anything behind."

"Did she know that you were going out on a date with me the following night?"

"Yes, I mentioned you frequently to Griselle. She offered to give us the private lesson at the studio."

Kema thinks, *Griselle was on a mission to sabotage our relationship. But let me not get too ahead of myself ... I'll give Victor a chance to finish his story.* Kema asks, "Did you and Griselle start dating?"

"Yes, we did but only after you wouldn't talk to me. It only lasted two months. She was possessive and too dependent on me for everything."

"Yeah, I think hanging panties in a bathroom that's not yours is a huge red flag for possessiveness."

They both laugh loudly as if time and circumstances haven't separated them.

"So, no I've heard the entire story. May I seek your assistance now?"

"Yes, you may Ms. Daniels."

Kema tells Victor about the low offer from Stellar Apparel and her proposal for a counter offer to them. He agrees to look over her paperwork and be present during the counter offer.

Victor chuckles and says, "Only Ms. Kema Daniels can have a major company acquire her business in the middle of a pandemic. You are a phenomenal woman."

*

Kema awakens an hour before her raucous cell phone alarm. Today is the day that Kema has the counter-offer meeting with Stellar Apparel. The video conference call is at 10:00 a.m. and Victor has booked the conference room at his office. Kema is pacing back and forth in her kitchen reviewing her talking points. Kema thinks, *I have to consider Stellar Apparel's point of view in this negotiation. Also, I have to emphasize that our company has been profitable and quickly adapted to the pandemic.*

Kema wishes that she could talk to someone right now to ease her nervousness. She looks at the clock on her microwave and it says 5:18. Kema knows she can't call anyone this early and decides to go back to her bedroom. Instead of getting into her bed and burying her head under the covers, she kneels and prays.

Lord, I'm feeling anxious. However, you say in your word that you have not given me the spirit of fear. You have given me love, power and a sound mind. Forgive me for not trusting you. Thank you for guiding my thoughts and discussion with Stellar Apparel. Amen

Kema goes back into the kitchen and prepares a cup of peppermint tea that she sips while checking her email. She takes a shower, puts on an ivory pants suit, black pointed toe heels, a pearl necklace and earrings. She combs her hair in a bun and wears neutral makeup to compliment her chestnut color skin tone. Kema sprays her neck with a citrus perfume that makes her feel confident and then she leaves her condo.

Kema arrives at Victor's office at 9:25 a.m. and he leads her into the conference room.

Victor turns away to leave the room but stops in the door-way as if he senses Kema questioning where he is going.

"I have a few loose ends to tie up in my office, but I'll be back in fifteen minutes. Would you like water, coffee or tea while you wait?"

"No, thank you."

Victor smiles and says, "You look and smell fantastic. Everything will work out."

Kema looks down bashfully and back up to respond, but

Victor has gone.

Kema smiles and thinks, *that man always says the right things at the right time.*

Victor returns to the room fifteen minutes later as promised and Kema goes over her talking points with him. Usually, Victor has a contrary point of view about her strategies, however, Kema is relieved that he agreed with her talking points.

Just before ten, Kema and Victor log into the video conference. Olivia Crenshaw, Peter Nicholson, the merger and acquisitions lawyer for Stellar Apparel, and three board members are already online.

"Good morning, all. I'd like to introduce my business attorney Mr. Victor Pennington who will advise me through the remaining proceedings."

Greetings follow before Peter cuts to the chase. "Well, let's get started, shall we? Ms. Daniels, would you like to present your counter offer?" Peter asks.

Kema nods. "As you know, Sweet Daddy's Fashions has weathered the storm of the pandemic by increasing its profitability when other retail stores have closed. Our online sales have exceeded in-store sales for four consecutive months. We have pivoted to becoming a PPE supplier to a local hospital as well as providing face masks to the local community. I understand we both want to receive the best deal possible. We have demonstrated our pliability and you will receive a dedicated team of employees with this acquisition. Therefore, my counter-offer is two million dollars."

Peter replies, "Ms. Daniels, I admire your passion and enthusiasm about your company. However, two million dollars is not a feasible price for this one retail store. We see that the store has promise and the most that we can offer is 1.2 million."

"Can we have five minutes to discuss this offer?" Victor inquires.

"Sure." Peter nonchalantly replies.

Victor turns off the video and mutes the sound on the computer. Feeling like that is not enough, he ushers Kema out of the conference room and into his office.

"Kema, I think you should take the offer."

"I aimed high asking for two million but I will settle for 1.5 million."

"Will you accept 1.2 million if I ask for Sweet Daddy's Fashions' employees to stay and the name of the company to remain the same?"

"I would like to maintain creative control of the Chicago store. Considering that they are acquiring this store I can negotiate a name change as long as it includes some portion of the original name."

"Sounds reasonable. I'll address your conditions once we get back on the video conference."

Victor and Kema walk back to the conference room and turn on the video and audio.

"My client will accept your offer of 1.2 million as long as the employees including workers that were brought in to assist with the PPE can remain with the company. In addition, my client would like to maintain creative control of the Chicago store. Lastly, she requests that some portion of the original name 'Sweet Daddy's Fashions' be included once the acquisition is final."

Before Peter Nicholson can reply, Olivia Crenshaw says, "I think your request is reasonable, Ms. Daniels. Your employees have proven to be loyal and should remain after the acquisition. It would make sense for you to maintain creative control of the Chicago store because you know your local clientele. We wouldn't want the store to completely lose its identity. Does the name 'Sweet Stellar Apparel' sound reasonable?"

"Yes, it does."

"I'll send the initial paperwork to Mr. Pennington," Peter says.

"Thank you. We'll review the paperwork and reach out to you if we have any questions."

Victor and Kema end the video conference. Victor grabs both of her hands, squeezes and kisses her on the check so as to reassure her that she made the right decision. Kema smiles warily remembering that she still has to tell her team.

CHAPTER 29

You could hear the sound of a feather drop to the floor of the store moments after Kema tells the team about the acquisition. Since everyone is wearing masks, Kema can only see bewilderment in their eyes. Darron finally breaks the silence and says, "I thought we were doing alright with the PPE contract and selling the face masks. Why do we have to sell out?"

Kema takes a deep breath before replying, "This is an opportunity that will benefit all of us. We will still keep our jobs. Once we are acquired by Stellar Apparel, we'll have additional resources to market the company and become more profitable."

"I'm sure we'll have to change our name to Stellar Apparel. How will our customers know that we're the same business?" Cassandra asks giving fuel to Darron's initial question.

"We won't have to change our name to Stellar Apparel. The CEO of Stellar Apparel recognizes that it is important not to alienate our customers. I'll still have creative control of the business. Also, the CEO has suggested the name 'Sweet Stellar Apparel' as our new name."

"I like the new name but it might take some time to get used to it. We won't be the Name Police patrolling the block to correct long-time customers for still calling us Sweet Daddy's Fashions," Antonio says.

The team laughs and the tension is broken.

"So ... are we all in agreement with the new name 'Sweet Stellar Apparel'?" Kema asks.

"Yes!" The team says in union.

"I wish we could have a party to let our customers know

about the name change. COVID is messing up everything," Pedro says.

"Hopefully next year we can do that. I'm picturing a block party with food, music and dancing," Jasmine replies.

"Okay, Pedro and Jasmine! It looks like both of you will be working closely with Monique Ewing, our event planner," Kema says with renewed enthusiasm.

Kema excuses herself from the group and goes to her office to sign the form for the name change. She checks that she has signed and dated each section before faxing the form to Victor's office. As Kema reviews the last page, she feels at peace, as if guardian angels have surrounded her. Her eyes rapidly scan her office, then she smiles as she sits back in her chair and thinks, *the storm is over.*

*

July 2021

We are 101.5 Chicago's #1 radio station on location at the long-anticipated block party for the grand opening of Sweet Stellar Apparel formerly known as Sweet Daddy's Fashions. Come out pick up a couple of outfits and enjoy some good food, music and dancing. We have DJ Pace spinning the hits. Let's go!

The block is filled with around three hundred people dancing and moving in an out of craft vendors' tents. Food trucks are lined up on the opposite side of the tents selling tacos, barbeque, hot dogs and hamburgers. As a result of COVID-19, there is no bouncy house at this block party and a few kids are walking with adults looking disappointed.

Kema is standing by the store's entrance as Janice and Julius approach her.

"Hey baby! Why are you standing by the door not enjoying yourself?"

"Hi Mama. Hi Julius. Oh! Excuse me. I should address you as the newlyweds. I didn't think you all would make it today."

"We decided to get some fresh air and check out the party. But we won't stay long," Janice replies as she turns her head and smiles deviously at Julius while caressing his face.

"Please Mama. This is a family function," Kema jokingly replies.

Julius laughs and says, "I know you're a grown woman and I can't tell you what to do, but I agree with your Mama. You should walk around and enjoy the party."

"I promise I will."

"Okay. Maybe we'll run into you again before we leave," Janice says.

Janice and Julius stroll away from Kema towards the food trucks. Kema walks toward the vendors' tents and sees Antonio and Natalie. Antonio is pushing the stroller of their one-year-old son.

"Hello Antonio! I'm glad you and your family made it. We've missed you in the store. How have you been?

"Hey Ms. Kema! I've missed y'all too. I'm doing good. I'm working as an IT specialist. The job has been demanding but today is for family since I have the day off. This is my fiancée, Natalie, and our son Antonio Jr."

"I have heard so much about you both and it's a pleasure to meet you," Kema replies.

"It's nice to finally meet you too. Thank you for encouraging Antonio to pursue his career goals."

"You're welcome. He was an integral part of my business and I wish nothing but the best for all of you."

"Ms. Kema. Watch your back. P.B. is running around this block party flirting with every woman in sight," Antonio cautions.

Kema laughs and says, "Thank you for letting me know. I'll be careful!"

"We've been here for about two hours and now it's time for us to go home out of this heat. Take care Ms. Kema," Antonio says, then begins to push his son's stroller.

As Kema watches the couple walk away, she is tapped on

the shoulder. She slowly turns around to see who it is as she prays that it isn't P.B. To her surprise, it's Joseph. He's wearing a fitted white polo shirt, dark blue jeans and white athletic shoes.

"Hello Ms. Kema. You look nice today. I mean you always look nice, but it's good to see you outside in casual clothes. This is a nice block party you've put together."

"Hello Joseph. Thank you. I can't take any credit for the party. Our event planner, along with Jasmine and Pedro, worked hard on it. Have you been here long?"

"About thirty minutes. I could have been here sooner but I was driving around ..."

Before Joseph could finish his sentence, Victor suddenly appears, grabs Kema around her waist, and says, "Hey Kema! I made it. Let's dance!"

Kema, looking wide-eyed, turns around to face Victor and says, "You almost gave me a heart attack. Also, you interrupted Joseph ...."

"I'm sorry that was rude of me. Hi, I'm Victor, Kema's boyfriend. Can I take her away for a moment to dance?"

"It's your world, man," Joseph replies dejectedly.

Victor takes her hand and the crowd around the elevated DJ booth parts as Victor and Kema approach. Victor guides Kema up to the booth and DJ Pace passes the microphone to him.

"Ladies and gentlemen. May I please have your attention? I want to take this moment to congratulate Ms. Kema Daniels on her grand opening of Sweet Stellar Apparel. She's a phenomenal leader and businesswoman. But I'm also on stage because I have a question to ask Ms. Daniels." Victor pulls out a small black box and drops to one knee and asks "Kema would you do me the honor of being my wife?"

The crowd erupts. Kema looks at Victor and then out into the crowd. She sees Janice, Julius and Sharon clapping in front of the DJ booth. She looks back at Victor with tears in her eyes and nods, saying "Yes".

"She said yes y'all! The party's not over. This song is for the engaged couple and all of the happy people out there," DJ

Pace says.

DJ Pace plays Maze and Frankie Beverly's classic party song *Before I Let Go* and some of the crowd forms a line dance. Victor and Kema remain on the stage and dance to the music. Kema has a tension headache from all the excitement of the day, but she is content.

Kema has found her happy place.

ACKNOWLEDGEMENT

I want to thank God for giving me the strength, creativity, courage, and discipline to complete this book. I am grateful for my mother, Mrs. Willie Dorsett, other family, and friends for their feedback and encouragement through this writing journey.

ABOUT THE AUTHOR

Shani Smith

Shani Smith has been writing since the second grade when she received her first diary. She wrote her first book in 2019 entitled I Didn't Part My Lips: Survival Strategies For Introverts Living In An Extroverted World. Her second book was published in 2020 and is entitled Sweet Daddy's Funeral. Shani has a Master of Science in Chemistry and a Master of Science in Cybersecurity Policy and Management. She lives in Mary-  land and enjoys reading, volunteering, dancing, cooking, and traveling.

BOOKS IN THIS SERIES

Kema's Story

Sweet Daddy's Funeral

Kema Daniels is a driven, ambitious professional who has dedicated her life to the pursuit of excellence. She is close to earning the biggest promotion of her career when her father, Benjamin Daniels, suddenly reenters her life after disappearing twenty-five years ago. During their reunion, she discovers aspects of her father's life that her mother, Janice wanted to remain hidden. After his death, she learns that her father left her with fifty percent of his clothing store, Sweet Daddy's Fashions. Kema is faced with making a decision that may affect her life: accepting the promotion or taking ownership of Sweet Daddy's Fashions.

Made in the USA
Las Vegas, NV
20 March 2022

45998232R00100